BOYS
of
BLUR

Also by N. D. Wilson

Leepike Ridge

Books of the 100 Cupboards
100 Cupboards
Dandelion Fire
The Chestnut King

Ashtown Burials
I: *The Dragon's Tooth*
II: *The Drowned Vault*
III: *Empire of Bones*

BOYS

of

BLUR

N. D. WILSON

RANDOM HOUSE 🏠 NEW YORK

Text copyright © 2014 by N. D. Wilson
Jacket art copyright © 2014 by Jon Foster

All rights reserved. Published in the United States by Random House Children's Books, a division of Random House LLC, a Penguin Random House Company, New York.

Random House and the colophon are registered trademarks of Random House LLC.

Visit us on the Web! randomhouse.com/kids

Educators and librarians, for a variety of teaching tools, visit us at RHTeachersLibrarians.com

Library of Congress Cataloging-in-Publication Data
Wilson, Nathan D.
Boys of Blur / N.D. Wilson.—First edition.
p. cm.
Summary: When his stepfather moves them to Taper, Florida, in the Everglades, twelve-year-old Charlie discovers a secret world hidden within the sugar cane fields, as well as new family connections and friendships.
ISBN 978-0-449-81673-8 (trade) — ISBN 978-0-449-81674-5 (lib. bdg.) — ISBN 978-0-449-81675-2 (ebook)
[1. Adventure and adventurers—Fiction. 2. Swamps—Fiction. 3. Sugarcane—Fiction. 4. Cousins—Fiction. 5. Stepfamilies—Fiction. 6. Family life—Florida—Fiction. 7. Supernatural—Fiction. 8. Everglades (Fla.)—Fiction.] I. Title.
PZ7.W69744Muc 2014 [Fic]—dc23 2013023615

Printed in the United States of America

10 9 8 7 6 5 4 3 2 1

First Edition

Random House Children's Books supports the First Amendment and celebrates the right to read.

This one is for Seamus James

(our life-loving laugh track)

BOYS
of
BLUR

When the sugarcane's burning and the rabbits are running, look for the boys who are quicker than flame.

Crouch.

Stare through the smoke and let your eyes burn.

Don't blink.

While cane leaves crackle and harvesters whir, while blades shatter armies of sugar-sweet sticks, watch for ghosts in the smoke, for boys made of blur, fast as rabbits and faster.

Shall we run with them, you and I? Shall we dodge tractors and fire for small handfuls of fur? Will we grin behind shirt masks while caught rabbits kick in our hands?

Shoes are for the slow. Pull 'em off. Tug up your socks. Shift side to side. Chase. But be quick. Very quick. Out here in the flats, when the sugarcane's burning and the rabbits are running, there can be only quick. There's quick, and there's dead.

ONE

MUCK

Out in the muck, where a sea of sugarcane stops and swamps begin, sitting beside a lake bigger than some countries, there is a town called Taper.

Taper has only one hill, a flat-topped mound just above the northern edge of town, ringed by cane. On that mound is an old white church with nothing but a stump where its steeple used to be before it was torn away by some long-forgotten hurricane. As for the church bell, it crashed through the floorboards and settled into the soft ground below. It's still down there, under the patched floor, ringing silence in the muck.

Most Sundays, the little church sees a few cars, and a minister under a wobbling ceiling fan preaching at old men and women who have heard it all before. But when this story starts, one of those men has moved right on beyond old and straight into dead. There's a whole herd of cars parked below that white church, and a whole herd of people standing around the rusty iron fence that cages in the graves.

The dead man's name was Willie Wisdom. And if he hadn't died, a boy named Charlie Reynolds might never have set foot on that mound in Taper, Florida, and this story would already have run dry of words.

Charlie Reynolds stood with his stepfather and his mother and his fidgeting little sister near the front of the crowd. From where he was standing, he could see loose black dirt mounded up on a tarp, ready to fill in a hole. He could see one end of the long box that held a man.

His neck itched. So he scratched it.

Charlie was not a boy who usually wore suits. And his neck wasn't the only place crawling with itches—just the worst of them. He had brown hair that went blond in the summer, a cluster of freckles on his nose that multiplied like weeds in the sun, and gold flecks in his hazel eyes in every kind of weather.

Normally, he wore old T-shirts and heavy shorts with deep pockets that were empty when he left the house in the morning and full when he returned at night. While he had a closet full of clothes and a dresser overflowing with shirts and pants that still smelled like store, he never touched them. He dressed from the laundry basket at the foot of his bed, and in the laundry basket he always found a T-shirt and a pair of shorts. On cold days, he added a raggedy hoodie that had belonged to his father.

Charlie hadn't worn a suit since his mother's wedding five years ago. He'd only been seven then, and he'd hated it, but he'd understood. Without the suit he couldn't hold the rings, and his mother had really, really wanted him to hold the rings.

For a moment, Charlie tried to pay attention. He looked at the flush-faced minister beside the grave. A sweaty roll of neck was bulging above his ministerial collar. For some reason, the man was talking about gardening.

Charlie couldn't listen. Not with the Florida sun shining and the wind rattling through miles of sugarcane fields and itches dribbling down his neck and in between his shoulder blades.

Not while he was sinking.

Charlie took a step back and stared at where he'd been standing—two wet footprints dented the turf on the hilltop. His stepfather's feet weren't making dents, they were making craters. Charlie leaned on one foot and bounced, testing just how far he could sink into the turf.

A hand landed on his shoulder and Charlie looked up.

Charlie's stepfather, Prester Mack, knew how to wear a suit. Big square shoulders, brown skin a little slick in the sun, he looked down at Charlie and shook his head no more than a centimeter, then let go of Charlie's shoulder.

Charlie knew his stepfather's football knees would be hurting, but Mack was tough, and the old man sealed in the box ready to go down into the hole had been the closest thing to a father Mack had ever had.

The minister was talking about bones now, a whole valley full of them. More than in the muck, he said. More than in a thousand fossil beds. His voice sounded like he was almost done.

Charlie inhaled slowly and the air tasted charred. He turned. A tower of smoke was roiling up from the fields.

Some people didn't care that old Coach Wiz had died. They had sugarcane to burn.

Three women sang.

Six big men stepped forward and lowered an old coach into the ground.

Willie Wisdom, foster father to twenty-seven, head football coach of the Taper Terrapins for thirty-two years. Rest in peace.

The crowd shifted and frayed around the edges. Men and women were hugging Mrs. Wiz where she sat by the grave in a white plastic chair. People were setting food on tables in the shade beside the church. A man was clattering glass Coke bottles into a little plastic swimming pool full of melting ice.

"You ever drink one from a bottle?" Charlie's mother asked. He looked up at her and shrugged.

"If you had, you'd remember."

Natalie Mack smiled at her son, but the smile didn't reach her eyes. Real smiles brought creases to the corners. Her look bounced away through the crowd before taking in the tower of smoke and then returning to Charlie.

"Mom?" Charlie asked.

His mother didn't answer. Standing barefoot in the grass, she dangled her high heels from one hand and Charlie's sister, three-year-old Molly Mack, from the other. Today and every day, his mother's hair was pulled back into a high doubled-over ponytail, but it seemed blonder than normal above her black dress.

As Charlie watched her eyes, he felt something tighten in his chest.

Charlie had been four when he'd learned how his mother's eyes looked when his father was on his way home. He'd been four the first time his mother hid him behind pillows on the top shelf of a closet. Five the first time he'd called the police. Five when he'd felt his first broken rib. Five when he'd learned to keep his face empty and five when his mother had loaded his backpack, taken his hand, and led him out the front door of their little house, past the rusted swing set, past his bike and his sandbox and an old worn football in the grass, and down the cracked sidewalk toward the bus station, never to return.

For a while after that, his mother's eyes had always looked the way they did when Charlie's father was on his way home, like he might be waiting around every corner, in every motel, in every restaurant, or walking behind them on every street.

Charlie had been six when his father had caught up with them, but by then, Mack had been there, too. Mack had changed everything.

"Mom?" Charlie asked. "What's wrong?"

Natalie sighed. Her eyes were on Mack, where he was laughing with three other old football men in the crowd. She shook her head. "Nothing." She smiled again, forcing eye creases this time. She cocked her hip and tugged Molly up onto it. "We'll be leaving soon, so make sure you eat something."

Charlie nodded. Molly looked at him, widening her brown eyes and making a big fake surprised face. Then she curled her lip into a snarl—her very best monster face.

Charlie gasped silently in fear. His sister laughed and threw her weight at the ground until her mother set her back down.

"I know you, Charlie," his mother said. "Wander if you like, just don't go far." Molly grabbed her mother's hand and began to drag her away. "And eat something!"

Charlie ignored the food tables. He slipped past church ladies in hats, men in suits, and clusters of boys slouching in red and white jackets. Each jacket had a football patch on one shoulder and a nickname on the back. Charlie saw ROCKET and SLIDE, J.TAG and WEAZEL. Free of the crowd, he moved through the taller grass, down the shallow side of the mound until only a narrow ditch in the black silt held him back from the cane fields.

The sugarcane looked like giant grass, bundles of green sticks taller than men tufted with long dry leaves like scythe blades. Separated by narrow, dark gaps, the rows marched away beneath the quiet blue sky. Not far from where Charlie stood, the sky's belly was rough with swamp trees. The fields and the trees both ended at the foot of a steep grass-covered dike—an earth wall taller than the white steepleless church and its mound combined.

A breeze slid around Charlie and on through the cane. The air was warm, but the field shivered like an old man with a chill.

Charlie looked at the sky, held up by nothing more than the column of smoke he'd noticed during the service. The flats were wide open, but he still felt strangely enclosed. He felt like he was standing at the bottom of a deep hole, a hole so wide the sky came all the way down inside it.

He didn't mind.

Charlie was in the cane where his stepfather had been raised and played his first football. Over the dike and across the water, he knew he would find more cane and the town of Belle Glade, where his real dad had been raised and played *his* football.

Both of his fathers had roots in the muck. Maybe Charlie did, too.

"Hey," a boy said behind him. "I guess we're some kind of cousins."

Charlie turned, squinting against the sun. The boy was thin, black, and about Charlie's height. He was wearing a creased red tie with an untucked dress shirt, canvas sneakers, and jeans. His hair was short, his eyes were big, and his smile was wide.

"I'm a Mack," the boy said. "Your stepdad is my pop's coz. So you and me are, too."

"Not really," Charlie said. "That would make us, like . . . step–second cousins."

The boy shook his head. He took one step and jumped, gliding over the ditch and landing lightly in the cane field.

"Nope," he said. He stripped the leaves from one of the cane stalks and snapped about a foot from the top. He broke it in two over his knee. "Cousins is cousins." He tossed one of the pieces to Charlie. "Try it."

Charlie examined his cane. Where it was broken, the end was gritty and wet with what looked like sap. He nibbled at a green corner. It tasted like sugar. Tiny bits of cane grit crept across his tongue.

"It's sweet," he said.

"Sweet?" The boy grinned. "Naw! Not sugarcane." He laughed, gnawed at the end of his own hunk, and then pointed it at Charlie. "Call me Cotton. Everybody does. I already know you're Charlie. I even know that your pops was Bobby Reynolds from Belle Glade who went to jail, but just about everybody knows that. You go to school?"

Charlie nodded.

"I'm homeschooled. My mom's crazy for books. Stacks and stacks of books I'm supposed to read and that's about it. And I can't play football." He tapped his sugarcane against a wide smile. "But I will. Next year I'll play. You play football? You fast, Charlie Reynolds?"

"Fast enough," Charlie said. "But I've never played."

Cotton exhaled disbelief. "You've got Bobby Reynolds for a pop and Prester Mack for a step, and you don't play?"

"Not yet," Charlie said. He prodded the sticky end of his sugarcane with a fingertip.

"But you will?"

Charlie shrugged. "It's my dad's sport. Both my dads."

Cotton chomped on his stick, studying Charlie. Finally, he dropped it in the trough.

"You scared of snakes?" Cotton asked.

Charlie shook his head.

"Good. Come on, I'll show you something." Without waiting for an answer, Cotton began running along the edge of the field, rattling through the leafy fringe.

Charlie dropped his cane hunk and hopped the ditch. When he landed, the damp muck rose around his feet. The first steps were the hardest but none of them were easy, and Cotton kept going faster. Charlie fought to stay in his new cousin's wake, thumping his shoulder against cane and turning his face away from brittle, slashing leaves, tugging every step up from the sucking ground.

After forty yards, Cotton suddenly veered, disappearing into the wall of cane.

Charlie followed. Cotton had turned into a narrow dirt road exactly one truck wide. The cane leaned in on both sides.

"Hey!" Charlie shouted. "Where we going?"

Cotton laughed and kept moving. His feet were lighter than Charlie's, barely touching the ground. Where Charlie planted and pushed, Cotton quick-stepped, floating into the air, gliding between the tire tracks and soaring over puddles. Charlie was quick enough, and he had never been clumsy, but trailing Cotton made him feel like a bulldog puffing after a greyhound.

Cotton turned again, and this time the road ran beside a ditch full of black water. Up ahead, something that looked like a busted old tire slid off the bank and splashed into the ditch.

Charlie wanted to stare at the water and get a better look at his first gator, but Cotton was still moving.

One more turn, and then trees. Cotton slowed and stopped. Charlie staggered up beside him, wiping his face on the sleeve of his suit coat. He was breathing hard, grass cuts stung his hands, and at least one blade had nicked his face. Cotton didn't seem to be breathing at all.

A narrow grass strip ran between the cane field and a deep canal. On the other side of the canal, thick swamp forest overwhelmed the bank. Ahead, a three-foot-high mound ran out of the swamp, bridged the canal, and disappeared into the cane. Swamp brush and scraggly trees crossed the canal on the mound's back and even grew out in the cane—a finger of wild stretching into tamed fields.

"This is it?" Charlie asked. "This is what you wanted to show me?"

Cotton's eyes were hooded. "The trees have been creeping," he said. "A lot longer than I've been alive. The mound has a stone core—tractors can't till it."

Cotton scrambled onto the mound. Charlie followed, grabbing slender trunks as he did. The ground was suddenly firm beneath his feet and with just that little bit of elevation he could see over the cane—the narrow mound ran through the field directly toward the little white church on its hill.

Cotton was moving again. Charlie turned and followed him along the top of the mound toward the swamp.

"Old shacks back in there," Cotton said, pointing toward the trees. "Shacks for cane workers—Haitians mostly. Now they just use tractors."

Cotton stopped over the middle of the canal, before they reached a wall of looming cypress trees slung with vines and bearded with moss. Charlie saw a snake on the far side slip down into the black water. The mound didn't just bridge the canal, it worked like a dam. On one side, a murky pool spread back into the trees, surrounding dozens of trunks. A tongue of water slid through a deep notch in the top of the mound and ran down into the canal on the other side. Cotton hopped the thin stream and crouched down.

At the boy's feet, embedded in the mound, was a chalky stone the size of a manhole cover but not quite circular. It was more egg-shaped. Cotton was scraping moss off the edges.

Charlie didn't care about the edges. Right in the middle of the stone, there was a dead snake, gray and speckled and twisted halfway onto its back. Beside it was a small dead rabbit.

"You killed them?" Charlie asked.

Cotton shook his head. "I didn't. I don't know who does. Sometimes I just think they come here by themselves when they're ready to die. Or someone collects them and leaves them here. There's always something, usually pretty small. Rats. Birds. Squirrels or skunks. Once they're here, nothing touches them. Nothing eats them." He looked at Charlie and lowered his voice. "When I found this stone, it was under moss and a whole pile of little bones."

He pointed into the trees at a short row of broken-down shacks. Only one still held up its own roof.

"I put all the bodies and bones in there," Cotton said. He looked at Charlie. "Wanna see?"

Charlie did want to see. And he didn't. The black water beside him and the looming trees and the chalk stone and the bones all felt very different from the cane fields with the white church on the hill beneath the blue sky and the sun.

"Well?" Cotton asked. Charlie nodded, staring at the collapsed and rotten shacks. And then something moved in the shadows.

Cotton picked up the snake by the tail and stood, grinning. "Wanna hold it?"

"Cotton," Charlie said, and he took a step back.

Cotton laughed and jiggled the snake. "Dead. See?"

A tall man stepped out from under the trees and into the light.

"Cotton!" Charlie grabbed his cousin and scrambled backward, smacking into a young tree.

Cotton dropped the snake and spun around. The man was walking toward them. He stepped onto the mound.

He was wearing a helmet.

He was holding a sword.

TWO COUSINS

Charlie winced and pulled away from his mother. The motel hand towel was rough and scalding on his face. Their room was small, but clean. Two beds were separated by a small antique table and a lamp.

"He's fine," Mack said. He'd taken off his jacket and tie, and his collar splayed wide around his thick neck. "Believe me, I've had enough of those cane leaf cuts to know. They sting, but they're just scratches."

Natalie Mack sat down on the motel bed next to her husband. She sighed. "You look like a cat attacked you, Charlie."

"Kitty cat!" Molly shouted. She climbed onto the bed behind Charlie and began to jump. Charlie shook with each impact.

"I'm fine," Charlie said. "They don't feel worse than paper cuts."

His mother winced with sympathetic pain.

"Be glad you had long sleeves," Mack said. He dragged a big hand down his face. He had worn a huge ring to the funeral—a state championship ring from long ago. It was golden rubbed down to nickel in places, with red colored glass pretending to be ruby. It was a dingy thing compared to the other rings Mack kept locked in a case at home, but it was the ring he'd won under Coach Wiz.

"A sword and helmet," Mack said. "You're sure the guy had a sword?" He'd already asked half a dozen times.

"I'm sure," Charlie said. "All rusty and jagged. The helmet was beat-up, too, but not as bad."

Mack's phone began to buzz in his pocket. He stood up and walked toward the door to answer it.

Charlie was left with his mother, her worried eyes, and her worried hands still fiddling with the wet towel. Molly climbed around her brother and dropped into his lap. She was talking to herself. Or her hands were talking to each other.

"You don't like it here," Charlie said to his mom.

She glanced around the simple motel room. "I'd rather be in Palm Beach, by the airport."

"I don't mean the room," Charlie said. "You don't like it *here*."

Molly put her small hand up over Charlie's mouth.

"Shhh," she said. "Monster coming! Hide!"

Charlie kissed his sister on the head, then she dropped

to the floor and raced toward the window to hide in the long curtains.

His mom smiled. "Coach Wiz meant a lot to Mack. I was happy to come. I'll be happy to go. No one ever threatened my son with a sword in Buffalo."

"He didn't threaten me," Charlie said. "He was just there."

Mack finished his call. He leaned against the wall with his big arms crossed. "I think Charlie and I are going to grab a Coke," he said. "Come on, Char."

As he turned toward the door, Molly exploded out from behind the curtains.

She wanted a Coke, too. She needed a Coke. She had to have a Coke.

Molly's muffled sadness followed her brother down the hall even after the door had closed behind them.

Then a television turned on, and sadness became joy.

Charlie trailed his big stepfather as they descended the stairs, passing a gargling vending machine on a landing. Two stories down, Mack led Charlie around a pair of plastic plants and through the lobby. No one was behind the front desk, but someone had propped a handwritten card against an old bell.

Five minutes later, Charlie and his stepfather were leaning against a propane tank in a gas station parking lot. The sun was down. Evening sky blues were turning to black. Charlie held a cold can between his hands, but

Mack's drink was in a brown bag. Neither of them had said a word since they'd left the room. Charlie didn't mind. Their best times together rarely involved words.

Charlie took a swallow and listened to the liquid squelch down his throat. The town of Taper was still. The air was still. The cane one hundred yards behind them wasn't even rustling. A laugh, blocks distant, trickled to them over the broken asphalt. A dog bark chased it away.

"Cotton made it home fine," Mack said. "That was his mama called me at the motel."

Charlie stared at his can. He hadn't even worried about Cotton. Out in the cane, Cotton had seemed faster than a rabbit.

"Funny thing," Mack added, studying the brown bag in his hand. "He didn't say anything to her about a man with a sword. Said he just told you some stories and messed with a snake and then you spooked."

"What?" Charlie blinked. Confusion bubbled into outrage. His stepfather was looking down at him with eyebrows up. "Why would he say that? I wouldn't run from a snake."

Mack looked up at the dark sky.

"I didn't make it up," Charlie said.

Mack set his drink on the propane tank behind him. "A lot of people see things in the fields, Charlie. You know why?"

"I wasn't seeing things!" Charlie shouted. "I—I . . . Cotton's lying."

"Do you know why people see things?" Mack asked again. Charlie shut his mouth and waited for the answer, certain he wasn't going to like it. "Because," Mack said, "out in the fields, there are a lot of things to see."

He tapped his old ring against the propane tank, then turned toward the dim wall of cane behind the gas station. Above the field, one vertical stripe of sky was darker than the rest. Another column of smoke. Another field burning.

"I ever tell you about my brother?" Mack asked, glancing at Charlie. "Herman Mack. Boy was fast. A lot faster than I ever was. Scrawn Lightning, Wiz called him."

Mack twisted the ring on his finger, old rhythms creeping into his voice, rhythms that had dropped away years ago. "We were running rabbits in a burn, took some rich white college boys out who had heard stories and wanted to see it. Herman could churn, and never faster than when a crowd was watching. So this big cottontail lights out like it has wings, quicker than any little muck fluff, and Herm's right on it, zigging and zagging, muck flying. They jump a canal to the next burn over, where the harvesters are already rolling. In the water, out of the water, and then over again. Finally, this thing shoots back into its home cane with the leaves still blazing. Herman smashes in after it."

Mack inhaled slowly, collecting himself. Charlie waited.

"No wind that day and the smoke was sittin' low. I could barely see him, but I'm sure people heard that scream all the way in Belle Glade." Mack looked at Charlie. "It's not just rabbits that bolt the burns. Fire pushes every breathing creature out that doesn't wanna get dead. Even the snakes. Herman got his hands on the rabbit, but his chest landed on a big old diamondback."

Mack reached out and tapped Charlie's right cheekbone with two thick fingers. "Big snake. More than six feet even after the head was off him. Hit my brother right in the face. Fang in his cheek, fang in his eye."

The night was cool and quiet, but Charlie's heart was pounding. He couldn't breathe.

"He should have died right then and there with that rabbit quiet in his hands." Mack looked at Charlie. "But he didn't. The white boys were screaming. I went for the snake. Then this old man comes out of nowhere, parting the smoke like a ghost. He tosses me away like I'm nothing, and he has that snake's head off quicker than I can see. Before I could even start to think, he'd sent those white boys running for the harvesters, and he had Herman's face split wide open and was sucking out blood and snake juice.

"The dude had skin like midnight, a big beard, and a string of rabbits hanging down his back." Mack looked at Charlie. "Strangest part was that he was wearing an old Spanish helmet with points turned up at both ends and an

21

old rusty sword tucked into a gator skin belt that still had the legs on.

"After a time he stood up, took the cottontail out of Herman's hands, let it hop off, then walked on past me without a glance. A big work truck bounced through the smoke right after he was gone." Mack smiled slightly. "That was more than twenty years ago, Charlie, but that's how I know you aren't making things up."

Charlie set his can down next to Mack's brown bag.

"What happened to your brother?"

Mack massaged his jaw. "Herman lost the eye, but something else was gone, too. He had fear he'd never had before, and his mind was always somewhere else. Dropped out of school, and a few years later, when your father and I were off knocking helmets in college, Lake O took Herman out of a little fishing boat with a storm."

Mack grabbed Charlie's can and his own brown bag and started across the rough asphalt toward two old gas pumps and the trash can in between.

Charlie heard tires hum, and then he saw headlights. A beat-up red truck bounced into the parking lot between Mack and Charlie and stopped outside the gas station door. Throbbing music shook the truck's mirrors as boys in red and white jackets tumbled out of the bed. The last to hop the tailgate was a tall white kid with slicked-back hair and huge fake diamonds in his ears.

The name on his jacket said SUGAR.

"Yo!" Sugar said. "Prester Mack!"

Every boy stopped. Every head turned to the man by the trash can.

Mack smiled, and the pack of boys parted as he walked back to Charlie.

"It true?" Sugar called after him. "Principal Laffy was talking you up after the funeral. We gonna be calling you Coach?"

Mack stopped beside Charlie and turned back around. He slapped one hand on Charlie's shoulder and pointed the other at the boys.

"Stay right with your brothers," Mack said. "Stay right with the Lord. Hit like thunder, and run . . . ?"

"Run like the devil's nightmare!" the boys all shouted.

Sugar grinned. "You already sound like Coach Wiz."

"Storm on, Taper," Mack said.

"Storm on!" the boys bellowed, and they bounced and laughed their way into the gas station, clattering a little silver bell against the door with every passing body. But Sugar didn't move. He stood alone beside the truck and stared at Charlie, his smile fading, his eyes hard and curious. And then Charlie felt Mack's hand on his shoulder, and his stepfather turned him around.

Charlie and Mack headed back toward the motel in silence. After a block, Charlie heard the truck tires squeal away behind them.

Mack cleared his throat. His face was lit faintly blue by

the motel sign. "That was something Coach Wisdom used to say."

Charlie didn't answer.

"He had a lot of things like that. Didn't matter if it was practice or just dinner or homework or curfew, he had sayings for everything."

Charlie nodded.

Mack sniffed at the air. "I haven't committed to anything yet," he said. "I was going to talk to your mom tonight."

"Mom doesn't like it here," Charlie said. "At all."

"She doesn't like what came from here. That's in the past now. Mostly."

"It's my dad, isn't it?" Charlie asked. "He's here?" He knew the answer already. He'd seen his mother's eyes at the funeral. He'd seen the old worry.

Mack nodded. "Not in Taper, but he's around. Working the sugar." He looked down at Charlie. "Would you be okay? Being here for a couple months? They only asked me to coach out the season. After that, if you hated it . . . well, we could talk."

"It's flat," Charlie said. "And you can't see the lake. It's weird being right beside a huge lake and not being able to see it."

"More snakes, too," Mack said. "But better football if I decide to start coaching. Much better football."

"And crazy people with swords." Charlie kicked a rock and watched it skitter off into the darkness.

Mack laughed and kicked a rock after Charlie's. "Don't you lose any sleep over him, Charlie Boy. You could find plenty of things here not to like, but he ain't one of them."

✳ ✳ ✳

Molly was fighting sleep on a pile of blankets at the end of her bed. Cartoons were on, the sound low. Charlie was lying on his back on top of his bed, staring at the uneven plaster on the ceiling. He could hear Mack's voice through the door that linked the two rooms.

Mack had grown up in Taper. He belonged here. What Charlie wasn't sure of, had never been sure of, really, was where he belonged. Where would he say that he had grown up? When he'd been much younger, back when his mother had still been with his father, they had moved around a lot, chasing every chance his father had at a football career. Charlie could remember different houses at Christmas, with lights up and his mother laughing. He remembered different streets with the same falling golden leaves, and the rustle and crackle as he kicked those leaves around his knees. Charlie had belonged in those moments—that's why he'd saved them. But he hadn't belonged in any of those places. Not for long.

The last few years, Charlie had lived with Mack and his mother and sister in a big new house in Buffalo, New York, with thin brick glued to the front like a disguise, and too many rooms all painted the same color of cream. It was on a big new street lined with big new houses just like it, where the neighbors took turns putting FOR SALE signs in their yards.

He didn't hate it. But it wasn't him.

Charlie sat up on the motel bed. He could hear his mother's voice now, loud and quick. He grabbed the remote off the bed and turned up the cartoons. Molly stirred.

Something tapped on his door.

Charlie stared. Someone had the wrong room.

Three more taps. Charlie slid off his bed and tiptoed to the door. Holding his breath, he looked through the peephole.

Cotton Mack stood in the hall. He was wearing shorts and a denim jacket with patches over a white T-shirt. His eyes darted up and down the hall, then he tapped on the door one more time.

Charlie opened it.

"Hey," Cotton said. "I want to show you something."

"You lied," Charlie said. "You said I made up the guy with the sword."

Cotton grinned. "I didn't exactly lie and I didn't exactly tell the truth. If I told my moms about that dude,

I wouldn't be here right now. Coz, if she knew half the things I see, I wouldn't just be homeschooled, I'd be locked-up-in-my-room-schooled."

Charlie was confused. "What did you tell her?"

"I said we didn't see nothing," said Cotton. "And she told me to speak proper English, and I said I was. . . ."

Cotton raised his eyebrows at Charlie. When Charlie didn't respond, Cotton just shook his head and sighed. "Double negative, coz. We *didn't* see *nothing*. Means we did see something. Now come on, let's go."

Charlie looked back into his room. Molly was snoring. His eyes settled on a pad of paper beside the phone.

"Hold on a sec."

Charlie traded his suit pants for an old pair of pocketed shorts and dug his hoodie out of his bag. Then he kissed Molly, adjusted her blanket nest, and hurried toward the door.

He left a note on the floor.

※　※　※

In the motel parking lot, Cotton climbed onto a rusty BMX bike. Fat pegs stuck out of either side of the rear wheel. Cotton pointed at them. Holding on to his cousin's bony shoulders, Charlie stepped up and on.

Cotton pushed forward, wobbled with Charlie's extra weight behind him, and then pumped them out of the parking lot and into the darkness.

"Where are we going?" Charlie asked. It seemed like something he should probably have asked sooner.

"Back to the graveyard," Cotton said. *"He's* there. And we're gonna get a better look."

He? Cotton could only mean the man with the sword. *In the graveyard? At night?* Charlie could have hopped right off the bike and walked back to the motel. He could have objected or argued or acted scared. He probably should have been scared.

But he wasn't.

The bicycle pegs swayed beneath Charlie's feet. He felt strange moving so quickly while standing so still, like a man in a chariot. Gravel crunched beneath the tires and Cotton's shoulders rocked under his hands. Moonglow loomed on the horizon. Or maybe it was the sky-kiss of distant city lights. Charlie's skin prickled as night air parted around him. Every bit of him was hungry to feel and to remember.

Florida darkness washed over him, and Charlie Reynolds filled his lungs with it. Maybe he didn't belong in this place, but he belonged in this moment. It smelled like rich earth and hidden water. It smelled like fire.

DIGGING FOR WISDOM

Breathing hard, Charlie wriggled up the hill beside Cotton. Tall, damp grass traced wet lines on his cheeks. His knees and elbows sank into the soft ground.

A yowl rolled through the darkness and over the cane fields.

"Panther," Cotton whispered.

The white church with the stumped steeple rose into view, now pearly with moon-silver. A breeze dragged quiet fingers across the back of Charlie's neck and his skin sprang into bumps. Shaggy cane heads rustled, passing the moon's light across acres of bladed sea, brushing the light up and away, defending the low shadows.

The yowl came again. Longer. Closer.

Cotton and Charlie peered through the graveyard's iron bars at the small grove of stones that marked the planted dead. Every stone was painted with moonlight. Every stone left a long stripe of night shadow behind it.

Charlie could hear the crunch and scrape of a blade biting through earth and hitting something hard, but he couldn't see around the nearest headstone. He leaned closer to Cotton, shoulder to shoulder.

A man was up to his ribs in Coach Wisdom's grave, and he was digging. The moon shone on his strange helmet, and on his dark sweat-slick skin.

Charlie felt his throat clamp shut as the man in the grave stopped digging. He sniffed the air and turned, his face only feet above the ground.

Through the rows of stones, his eyes met Charlie's. They were liquid with moonlight, calm and unsurprised. Then the man's eyes moved on. They slid across the dim orange streetlights of Taper and settled on the jagged black tree line that marked the end of the cane and the edge of the swamp.

Cotton was sliding back down the hill, but Charlie grabbed his cousin's arm.

"He saw us!" Cotton hissed.

Charlie shook his head. He wasn't running this time, and he wasn't going to watch the rest alone.

The man in the grave was still staring at the trees. And then wind swept over the fields and washed up through the tall grass around Charlie and Cotton, carrying a smell so foul that Charlie pressed his face down into his sleeve. Cotton began to gag.

It smelled like gutted skunk, like rotten eggs and corpse and sewage. Like the deep slime bottom of a swamp, collected decay unstirred for a thousand years and then dredged up into the air.

And it made Charlie angry. He suddenly hated Cotton for being faster than he was. He wanted to hit him. He wanted . . . he wanted . . .

The man leapt out of the grave and tossed away his shovel. He drew his ancient rusty sword and dropped into a crouch, turning in a slow circle.

"*Bonswa kochon sal!*" the man shouted. "Begone! I do not fear *piti* demons. My feet of flesh are bare in God's *jaden!*"

On the far side of the graveyard, a dark shape rose slowly behind the fence. The moonlight did little to it. The man with the sword faced it, straightening slowly.

"You cannot be having him," the man said, pointing his sword into the grave. "I am Lio, *o diab!* Begone, or the grave ground curse you. Go back to your cage—*kote mò yo ye!*"

The shadow extended two dark arms, gripping the iron fence. Metal squealed and popped.

The man with the sword raised his blade and pointed straight at it.

A panther screamed in Charlie's ear.

Charlie yelled as the big cat sailed over him. Its tail snapped against his cheek and then the cat was across the fence and among the graves.

Another panther landed beside it. Both cats slid toward the shadow, hissing and spitting, fangs bare in the moonlight.

The shadow released the fence and retreated into the darkness. The cats launched after it, disappearing over the curve of the mound. The fence rocked quietly in the wind, bent inward where the shadow had been. The stench drifted away.

The man with the sword turned toward Charlie and Cotton. "I am Lio." He slid his sword back into his gator skin belt and picked up the shovel. "You must stay close with me until . . ." He gestured at the night. A scream rolled over the hill and rode away on the wind.

Lio jumped back into the grave and began punching his shovel straight down, cracking it against the coffin within.

"What are you doing?" Charlie stood slowly.

"Don't talk to him!" Cotton said, rising to his knees. "I don't know what that thing was, but he's digging up a dead dude. We have to get out of here, Charlie!"

Wood splintered and Lio bent down into the grave.

"Charlie!" Cotton shouted. "I can't be here!"

Lio grunted. More wood cracked. And then the body of a man in a suit rolled up out of the grave and onto the grass.

Coach Willie Wisdom.

Coach had not been a small man, but Lio hopped up beside him, dropped to one knee, heaved the body up onto his shoulder, and then stood.

A panther screamed in what could only be pain.

"*Vini ave'm!*" Lio grunted at the boys. "*Li ugen!*"

"No Creole!" Cotton said, raising his hands. He stood beside Charlie. "We're leaving."

"Stay close with me," Lio said. "Or your mothers may be weeping *nan maten.*"

Lio took long, quick strides around the gravestones, moving easily despite the weight of the dead coach over his shoulder, and then passed through the iron gate. Without a backward glance, he strode down the hill toward the cane.

Charlie looked at Cotton. They both turned, scanning the darkness around them. No more yowling or snarling. Nothing but the breeze rattling the cane like bones.

"Follow!" Lio shouted.

"No, sir," Cotton muttered. He backed away, eyes wide and white, then turned and ran toward the dim lights of Taper.

For one moment, Charlie was alone. Fear turned in his

gut and sent electricity racing through his skin. He wanted to run. He wanted to be under a heavy blanket inside a bright room with locked doors and closed curtains. But he could bottle fear. He'd been doing it his whole life. He could push it away and follow the man called Lio; he could ask about the panthers and the shadow and the stench and the anger it had made him feel.

Charlie shivered.

A foul ghost of reek touched his nostrils—a memory of that fence-bending shadow that his mind couldn't explain.

Or the first finger of its return.

Charlie sprang after Cotton. He lengthened his legs and filled his lungs and he ran.

The streets of Taper were empty. Leaning streetlights spread quiet cones of orange over hibernating cars and sealed storefronts.

Charlie's feet slapped on the asphalt as he ran down the center of the road. His chest heaved and his breathing was louder than the humming lights above him.

A shut-down diner. A liquor store. A barbershop. An antique store. A tiny theater. All quiet. Some forever.

"Hey!" Cotton jumped out from behind a parked car.

Charlie yelped in surprise and almost fell down.

"The sheriff will be nuts," Cotton said. "Everyone will be all up about some crazy grave-robbing Swamp John. I'm not gonna lie about him, but don't you go talking about that Stank. People think I'm crazy enough already."

Charlie panted. "We didn't see nothin'?" His laugh came out as a wheeze. "Double negative?"

Cotton shook his head. "This isn't funny, Charlie. This is cops and bodies and some serious spook."

Charlie nodded, still panting, and braced his hands on his knees.

"And next time, coz, don't be hanging back when things go all Hound of the Baskervilles," Cotton said, backing down the middle of the street. "That's when it's time to run."

"Hey, I was fine in my room," Charlie said. "You were the one who brought me. And I don't even know what a baskerville is."

Cotton turned toward a side street and broke into a jog. "Read a book, yo!"

"Whatever," Charlie said, but he was alone. He looked back over his shoulder. The street ran out of orange lights before it ran out of boarded-up buildings. At the end, there was an old half-broken barricade and a rusty sign puckered with bullet holes dangling sideways from a single screw.

DEAD END

Beyond the sign, swaying cane. In the distance, the little white church on the hill throwing quiet light back at the moon. Somewhere in the darkness, Charlie knew, a man was lugging a body. Somewhere, something with hands stronger than iron was creeping through the cane, trailing a smell as foul as hate itself.

Charlie ran.

※　※　※

Natalie Mack closed her eyes and splashed cold water on her face. With firm fingertips, she pressed the cold against her cheekbones and moved up to her brows.

It was supposed to relieve stress. But she wasn't feeling stress. She was just . . . nervous.

Four suitcases were already sitting by the motel room door. Molly was dressed and fed and laughing on her father's lap at the end of the saggy motel room bed.

Natalie allowed herself one quick look in the mirror above the sink. Her blond hair was in a pile on top of her head, spiked in place by a motel pen swiped from the pad beside the phone. Her eyes were clear and sharp. For some reason, she felt like they were supposed to be bloodshot.

She turned her head slightly, just enough to see the pale scar peeking out from behind her ear.

Somewhere in this broad, flat land of muck and cane, there was a man she had once loved, a man who had given her that scar, who had given her Charlie.

She blinked, pressed a towel against her face, and went to wake her son.

Charlie's shins and knees were smeared with dirt and grass. The arms of his sweatshirt were much worse—filthy from elbow to wrist. And he stank. The whole room smelled like horse. Or something less . . . alive.

Natalie bit her lip and leaned back against the doorjamb. She couldn't stop a smile. All in all, Charlie looked like a boy who had been having himself some fun.

"Charlie?"

Charlie jerked in surprise and slid up onto his elbows. "Hey." He left his eyes shut for a moment.

"Charlie? Are you okay?" He felt his mom's weight dip the mattress beside him. Her hand touched his face, her fingers immediately tracking the largest cane stripe across his forehead.

Charlie opened his eyes. "Yeah," he said. "How about you? Are you okay?"

Natalie smiled. A real one. Her eyes creased.

"Yeah, Charlie Boy, I'm fine. We're fine." She tugged on his filthy sleeve and her smiling face became a question mark. Charlie sat all the way up and pressed his back against the wall. A television was selling something on the other side of it.

"I'm sorry," Charlie said. "I shouldn't have gone out. But Cotton came by and you and Mack were talking. I thought Molly would be okay if I left the door to your room a little open." He studied his mother's face, but she wasn't giving anything away. "I left a note," he added.

Natalie nodded. "I got it. It's a small town, Charlie, but still, just taking off like that . . ."

"I know," Charlie said.

He watched his mother's eyes shift. The subject had just changed somewhere behind them.

"What did you and Mack decide?" he asked. His mother looked at him, surprised. "About coaching. About staying here."

"He told you?"

"Not exactly," Charlie said.

His mother's eyes narrowed. "What do you think?"

Charlie shrugged. "Mack wants to. You don't want to. And I don't get to vote."

Natalie smacked Charlie's shoulder and smiled, lips tight. "Mack would die for us, Charlie. I can die just a little bit for him. There's nothing for him back in Buffalo. He hates it. Showing up to sign jerseys for lines of old fans? Plus, he loves the idea of coaching you when you're a little older. *If* you want to play," she added quickly. "You don't have to. But you'd be great." She brushed a school of dirt crumbs off the bed. "I want Mack to be happy, Charlie. When I married him, I married his history, his roots, everything that makes him *him*. And when he married me—"

"He got a white kid."

"Don't sell yourself short." Mack stepped into the doorway, smiling as he spoke. "You've got some freckles."

"Molly and I are flying back to Buffalo to pack up some things," Natalie said to Charlie. "We'll be back down in a week. You can come with us or you can stay here with Mack."

"We're really moving here?" Charlie looked from his mother to his stepfather. "Seriously?"

Molly muscled her way into the room between Mack's knees.

"Through the football season," Mack said. "Then we'll see."

"What about school?" Charlie asked. "Can I skip the rest of the year?"

Natalie rolled her eyes.

"Homeschool me!" Charlie said. "Just sign me up with Cotton's mom. He's homeschooled."

Mack grinned. "Boy, you don't know what you're asking. Now, are you staying or going? Your mom could use you back home, but I could use you, too. Got to find a car, a house, everything."

Molly climbed up onto the bed, bounced once, and then stood, studying her brother. "Charlie, take a bath!" She pointed toward the bathroom. "Now! You take a bath!"

Charlie tried to think about Buffalo, about school and his bedroom and the bike he had left in the garage. But his mind slipped quickly back to the cane, to this place with the thick black muck and burning fields where both of his fathers had grown up, where Charlie had already seen things that he would never forget.

"I'll stay," Charlie said.

Mack nodded. Natalie kissed Charlie on the head, then messed up his hair. Molly poked him on one dirty kneecap.

The goodbyes were quick. Two suitcases left and two suitcases stayed. Charlie got into the shower and watched the night before wash off him, swirling in a miniature swamp between his feet before draining away into even deeper darkness.

The water cleared. The tub whitened. Steam flushed the last traces of that smell from his nostrils but not from his mind. It stuck to him like fear from a nightmare, like one of the dark scars in his memory that could never fade. He had buried those memories deep and left them undisturbed. But the stench on the mound had torn them loose. Feelings had exploded inside him without asking his permission, and their sour tracks still ached behind his breastbone.

Charlie shoved his face in the water. Feelings would go away. There were other things to think about. A new town. A week with Mack. Normally that would be exciting. But panthers? A grave robber? And that shadow . . .

Charlie tapped the faucet hotter and hotter until it was almost painful.

He was still there when the sheriffs banged on the motel room door.

COTTONMOUTH

Charlie jumped into fresh shorts and tugged a black T-shirt down over damp skin. He was alone. Mack and the sheriffs had already gone down to wait for him in the parking lot.

Charlie felt like hopping out the motel room window and taking off. But that wasn't a real option. He fought to get his socks onto his wet feet and then stepped most of the way into his shoes, crushing the backs under his heels. Good enough. He'd fix them later.

Charlie skipped the elevator and raced down the fire stairs two at a time, shoes flapping. He jogged through the lobby and banged through the glass doors into eye-watering sun. The day was already several shades past warm and he hadn't even had breakfast.

Blinking, Charlie threw his arm up across his forehead and focused on the shapes of three men beside a police car. Mack was wearing sunglasses and an old Taper Terrapins polo shirt. His veined and knuckle-scarred hands were on his hips. One of the cops was black. Short and solid, he wore a flat-brimmed trooper's hat. The other cop was white and even taller than Mack, though he hunched forward around a soft middle that teetered over his belt buckle. He was wearing a sun visor, jeans, mirrored sunglasses, and snakeskin boots. A fat red mustache reclined on his upper lip like an overweight caterpillar too tired to cocoon. On his right hand he wore two huge rings, and he was chewing gum.

"Charlie Reynolds!" the man said. He glanced back at the other cop and pointed at Charlie. "Am I seein' things? Don't he look like Bobby Reynolds?"

"Don't he just," the other cop said. He adjusted his belt and stared at Charlie.

"I'll say." The tall cop and his mustache leaned forward. "Holy Mother of Mo, you look like your daddy!" He stuck out his right hand. Charlie shook it. The hair on the back of the man's hand felt like old rug. His rings felt even bigger than they had looked. "I mean, you don't have half the bull meat on you that your daddy had, and you don't have his stringy hair, and you still need some inches on your bones, but all that can grow." He dropped Charlie's hand and straightened up, adjusting his belt. "What position you play? You got any speed?" He glanced back at the other cop and raised his eyebrows. "Bobby had *speed*."

"*Speed,*" said the other cop.

Mack stepped around behind Charlie and put his hands on his stepson's shoulders.

"Charlie, this tall talker is Sheriff Leroy Spitz, and that's Deputy Hydrant Landry behind him. They wanted to ask you a couple questions."

"Ho now!" Sheriff Leroy Spitz tapped up his sun visor and peered down at Charlie over his sunglasses. "Prester Mack wants us to get down to business. I get the impression that he'd like us to move along, Charlie. You getting that impression, too?"

"Hydrant?" Charlie asked, looking at the thick, shorter cop.

"That's right," said Spitz. "His mama called him Steven, but we all called him Hydrant. I mean, look at him. He used to knock your stepdaddy there flat on his all-state backside just by standing there."

"Don't know about that," Mack said.

"Sure," Spitz said.

"Sure," grunted Hydrant.

"Sure as I'm wearing rings," Spitz said. He held up his hand and wiggled his ring-cuffed fingers. "Here's the thing, Charlie. . . ." The sheriff dropped all the way into a crouch like he was talking to a little kid. Charlie stared down at him, confused and suddenly much too tall. The sheriff coughed, acted like he was stretching, and levered himself back up. "Thing is, Charlie, Hydrant and I played ball with your daddy. We whipped up on those Taper Terps and their Mack boys."

"Whipped 'em up," Hydrant said.

"And then we beat 'em on down." Spitz grinned and adjusted his visor. "Beat those scrawny little rabbit runnin' muck bunnies into fluff."

Charlie could feel Mack's hands tighten slightly on his shoulders. "You did," he said. "A school four times our size beat us down. Twice. My freshman year. My sophomore year. What happened the next two years?"

Spitz laughed and waved off Mack's question like a gnat.

"Sure, you got a couple wins, too," Spitz said. "But Bobby ran you out of the state. Hydrant, what did Bobby put on the Terps junior year? Two hunnies? Three?"

Hydrant cleared his throat and lifted his chin. "Two hundred and seventy-four yards rushing."

Spitz whistled. "That's something else." He pointed at Mack, but he was looking at Charlie. "Your daddy should've been the one off in the league, making millions. Your daddy, Charlie Reynolds, and don't you forget it." He looked at Mack. "Kinda strange, Prester Mack, you linking up with Bobby Reynolds's old lady like that. Raising his son."

"Strange," said Hydrant.

Prester Mack stepped around Charlie, big hands on his hips but an easy smile still on his face.

"This why you boys came?" Mack said. "Get some cracks in to my boy?"

Spitz wrinkled his mustache with half a grin. "You mean *Bobby's* boy?"

Hydrant stepped forward, sliding between the two taller men. They stared at each other over his hat. Mack pulled off his sunglasses.

"If you have any real business, I'd get to it." Mack's voice was riding on a growl. "If you don't, I'm likely to forget you're a cop."

Sheriff Leroy Spitz raised his hands and smiled at Mack. Then at Charlie.

"Played quarterback myself," he said. "People called me Firecracker on account of my red hair and my knowing how to light people up." He patted Mack on the shoulder and stepped around him. "Girls just called me Fire."

"Boys just called you Cracker," Mack said.

"That they did," Spitz said. He pulled off his sunglasses and winked at Charlie. His eyes were grimy blue. "Jealousy is a sickness." Reaching back, he snapped his fingers behind him. Hydrant tugged a little notepad out of his shirt along with a tiny pencil.

"You know why we're here?" Spitz asked.

Charlie nodded. Then he shrugged. Finally, he shook his head.

Spitz laughed. "Boy, don't ever get yourself arrested. You look guilty sideways to Sunday."

Charlie licked his lips, and as sweat sponged out of his forehead, he wiped it on the shoulder of his T-shirt.

"This morning, we got a call about René Mack," Spitz said. "Asked around a bit and heard you might know something."

Charlie blinked. He looked at Mack and then back at the sheriff.

"René? I don't know who that is. I've never met her."

Spitz grinned. "Not a *her.*"

"He means Cotton," Mack said. "His real name is René." He looked at Spitz. "What kind of call? What happened?"

"Wish we knew." Spitz pulled off his visor and wiped his head with his hairy forearm. "He never turned up home last night. His mama called us this morning. She calls us on him at least once a month, so we're not throwing any panic switches just yet, but the way things have been around Taper lately, we figured it might be best to start poking around."

"The way things have been?" Mack asked. "What do you mean?"

"All the runaways," Spitz said. "Been real high cross the whole county the last few weeks, and young ones, too."

"Too young," Hydrant said.

"Not talking about punks and dropouts," Spitz said. "Good kids. Twelve, eleven years old. Couple just ten."

"Ten," said Hydrant. He clicked his tongue and shook his head.

46

Charlie wasn't listening. Cotton was missing? Hadn't made it home?

"Charlie?"

He looked up into his stepfather's dark eyes. Mack nodded toward the sheriff.

Spitz cocked his head. "We got someone says they saw René jump out at you from behind a parked car last night just about where Dredge Street dead-ends. Says René took off running. Then you took off running. That right?"

Charlie swallowed. He bit his lip. Then he nodded.

Hydrant made a careful note—thick fingers pinching tiny pencil.

Spitz tugged his belt up against his belly. "Now what were you boys up to?"

"Cotton took me out in the cane. On his bike."

"Why?" Mack asked. "He trying to scare the city boy?"

"I guess," Charlie said. "But we both got spooked. He took off running and I followed him."

"Guess you don't have *speed*," Spitz said. He winked again.

Charlie blinked. So many things could have happened to Cotton. He could hear the panthers. He could smell that . . . stench. He could see that tall man with the body on his shoulder. What had the man said?

Stay close with me.

Your mothers may be weeping *nan maten.*

"I didn't follow him right away," Charlie said. How

much should he say? Charlie cleared his throat. "The moon was up. There were two panthers and this—"

"Heard them or saw them?" Spitz interrupted.

"Both," said Charlie.

Spitz glanced at Hydrant. "Bobcats more than like." He smirked at Charlie. "Plain ol' cats, maybe. Things look bigger in the dark, specially to a city boy."

Hydrant nodded and made a note.

Charlie wanted to argue, but he just shrugged. "Cotton ran. I ran. He jumped out when I was in the street. Said goodnight. Took off. I assumed he was going home."

Hydrant made another note.

"Right," Spitz said. "Well, I'm sure the boy will turn up when he's hungry. His mama probably set out some big pile of book uglies he didn't want to read. I swear she homeschools blisters on that boy. That's why he took off the last couple times."

Hydrant tucked his notepad and pencil carefully into his breast pocket. Then he crossed his hands in front of his belt like a soldier on guard.

Spitz moved toward the driver's side of the cop car and pulled it open. He hesitated.

"Last question, Charlie Reynolds. There's half a million acres of cane in this state. Where you boys go exactly? You have any idea?"

Charlie shifted, scraping his shoes on the asphalt.

There was no reason to lie. Was there? And he wouldn't lie to Mack. Still . . .

"Near the church." He cleared his throat. "That's where the panthers and . . . this . . . There was . . ." He exhaled and squinted in the sunlight. He shrugged. "It just got spooky."

Spitz nodded. He tapped his visor, stuck his glasses back on, and folded himself into the car. Then he pointed at Mack, but he was looking at Charlie.

"Don't be letting old bad knees Prester here tell you you're a Terp. You're a Reynolds and that makes you a Buccaneer, kid, and don't you forget it. A Bucc! It's in your blood."

The sheriff saluted. The engine started. Gravel crunched as the cop car rolled to the edge of the parking lot.

The driver's window slid down.

"Work on that *speed!*" Spitz shouted.

"*Speed!*" Hydrant bellowed.

Charlie and Mack watched the car bounce out into the street and pull away.

After a moment, Mack inflated his chest. And then his cheeks. When he exhaled, it all came out in a blast.

"Those guys are idiots." Mack looked up at the sky. "Charlie . . . your dad . . ."

Charlie looked at his stepfather. Mack never talked about Charlie's dad. None of them did.

"Not sure how to say this." Mack pulled off his sunglasses. He massaged the bridge of his nose, and then he met Charlie's eyes with his own. "Your mom wasn't crazy. To marry him. He wasn't always what he turned into."

"He doesn't matter," Charlie said. He looked away. Thinking about his dad made his chest feel brittle. Even the flashes of happy memory. Especially the happy memories. They made the bad memories worse. If he didn't change the subject in his mind, his throat would try to close and breathing would make his eyes water. And after last night, everything inside him was already too loose.

"Fathers always matter," Mack said. "In high school, I respected what he could do, and he respected me. He wasn't like Spitz. Then, in college, we were the only two Florida boys on our team. We were roommates. We were friends."

Charlie knew this already. He wanted to change the subject.

"Charlie Boy," Mack said. "Look at me."

Charlie hesitated. But he did. Mack's eyes were solemn.

"Your father made mistakes. We all do. But instead of working to set things right, he chose to protect those mistakes—he let them be. He even fed them, which made them so much worse. Mistakes don't just hang on the wall like ugly pictures. Mistakes are seeds." He thumped his chest. "In here. They grow. They take over. You make a mistake, you gotta make it right. Dig that seed out. Old

Wiz used to say, 'Fruit rots, wood rots, but lazy-ass boys rot the fastest.'"

Charlie exhaled. Then he nodded.

"Now, here's the thing," Mack said. "Your father hurt you and your mother in every kind of way. His mistakes are yours to overcome, but they don't need to grow in you. You'll make plenty of your own." Mack smiled and his eyes warmed. "But your daddy's cane-fire speed? His wildcat toughness? His laugh? That stuff is in your genes, kid. Yours to keep and yours to grow with sweat and effort. Bobby Reynolds squandered it all, but you don't have to. If those things rot, it will be on you and me. Not him. Not anymore." Mack thumped Charlie on the shoulder. "Got it?"

"I'm not that fast," Charlie said. "Or tough."

Mack grinned. "You think I haven't seen you run? Kid, you're a long way from slow, and you were already tougher at six than most at eighteen, though I wish you hadn't needed to be."

Toughness. Speed. More thoughts Charlie didn't want to think. He pushed his mind back to Cotton. His cousin was somewhere in the quiet morning heat. So long as he hadn't been caught by that . . . *stink*. Or a panther. But maybe the cops were right and he was just hiding from his mom.

"Is Cotton's name really René?" Charlie asked.

Mack laughed. "It is. French, and not a girl's name over

there. His mama always wanted her boy to be all brain. Said muscles were only good for slaves, so she named him after someone famous for thinking."

"But why does she call him Cotton?" Charlie asked.

Mack smiled. "That kid was three years old when some punk told him he had a girl's name. From that moment on, he wouldn't answer to it. Named himself Cottonmouth and that was that and no discussion. *Cotton* must have been time's compromise." Mack stretched his arms above his head, talking through a yawn. "Okay, Charlie Boy, I need breakfast and about ten gallons of coffee. Then we buy ourselves a car, I meet with the superintendent, and you can find your mom and Molly the house of their dreams."

"What kinda dreams?" Charlie asked. "Nightmares?"

Mack laughed, ruffled Charlie's hair with a heavy hand, and then shoved him away. Charlie slipped out of his shoes and hopped in socked feet on gravel. Mack was already walking away.

Charlie grabbed his shoes, unflattened the heels, and tugged them all the way on.

A long, sharp whistle sliced back to Charlie as Mack disappeared behind a low brick building. He was acting more like a coach already.

With shoelaces loose and their whip-tips clicking, Charlie raced after his stepfather.

❋ ❋ ❋

Pastor Steve Beaux Revis was running late. It happened sometimes on weekdays, but it was never pleasant arriving at the church when the elderly early risers who made up the congregational steering committee and ladies auxiliary union were already gathered around the locked door of the sanctuary, watching him fumble with his keys with their eyebrows raised, winking wrinkled lids at each other as they all loudly agreed that young growing boys needed their sleep.

He was forty-eight years old, for goodness' sake. He had two boys in college and his wife had been in the little graveyard for three years. But to his ancient congregation, a heavyset middle-aged widower was just another kid from the cane.

Pastor Beaux pulled his battered sedan to a stop at the bottom of the hill. So far, so lucky. The cars were all parked, but no white-haired shapes lurked by the church door, leaning on canes. He must have left the building open after the funeral. He hopped out and climbed the mound.

The front door was locked. No doubt his esteemed elders found that hilarious. His key required less jiggling in the church door than normal, and the iron hinges complained as loudly as ever when the door swung open.

Two steps into the sanctuary Pastor Beaux stopped, his heavy feet on the rough board patching the hole where the old church bell was buried. The place was empty. And something was wrong with the light. It was slanting into the room through a row of white windows as it always did, warming dust motes and pews. But there were shadows. He walked slowly down the aisle, looking at the windows. Dark stripes had been painted across every pane of glass.

Pastor Beaux ran out of the church, and puffed around the building and into the graveyard. His feet and his breath stopped at the same time.

Old men and women were standing among the tombstones, staring and whispering. Beaux hardly noticed. A huge symbol—crescents and circles and swooping lines—had been painted on the side of the white church, crossing windows and stretching from near the ground all the way up to the roof. The paint was dark red, almost black, the color of dried blood.

Pastor Beaux turned slowly, moving his eyes from the wall down into the graveyard, to the grave where he had been standing yesterday, to the grave that should have been holding the body of the old man who had taught him just about everything he thought he knew.

Dirt mounds lined the sides of the open grave. The fresh headstone had been knocked back onto its granite heel.

Reaching up out of the grave, sinewy and knotted like a serpentine muscle, a black ironwood tree was growing.

It couldn't be. But it was.

Pastor Beaux walked toward the grave like a dreamer.

He looked down into the hole at the splinters of the very empty coffin. The tree had somehow grown up through the coffin's bottom. Threads from torn white satin cushions were tangled around the trunk and snagged on the rough bark. Ironwood leaves fluttered level with the pastor's head.

Coach had been replaced with a tree.

A live tree. Pastor Beaux leaned out over the grave and grabbed the trunk. The wood was rock hard and cool against his palm. He tugged. It was rooted. And iron solid.

RUNNING THE RABBITS

Charlie sat on the grass with his legs spread out, his back pressed against the red cinder block wall of the locker room. Most of his body managed to be in the shade. He was tired. He was hungry. And his mind wouldn't turn off.

On the field in front of him, high school boys yelled. Whistles chirped. Pads crunched. And Mack's voice bellowed above all the rest. A few people were scattered through the bleachers, sitting in the full sun, there to watch the great Prester Mack run his first practice. Small groups of men huddled along the edges of the field for the same reason. At first, Charlie had cared what they were saying. But it had all been the same.

Boy's been struggling. He turn it around?

Dunno.

He just might turn things around.

Sure enough. If he don't, who could?

Dunno.

Think he'll turn it around?

Charlie's eyes shut slowly. The sun had simmered down his energy. And all the walking. No, not so much the walking. It was all the stopping and talking. They'd walked from the motel to a grimy little diner with just a few customers and a flock of flies so slow and heavy that Charlie figured Molly could have rounded them all up in five minutes. Charlie had wanted to tell his stepfather about Cotton, about the grave, about what he had seen. But it wasn't an easy story to start, and once Mack was in the diner, customers had packed in after him and all of them had been loaded with questions. Charlie had eaten his pancakes and watched Mack prod his waffle for more than an hour without five minutes to chew sprinkled through it. When they had walked to the little gravel lot to look at the used cars the town of Taper had to offer, at least half the crowd had followed them.

There had been only five cars for sale, all of them battered, all with huge bright yellow price stickers followed by exclamation marks. The two saddest were minivans bedecked with sagging balloons on each side mirror.

Despite the excitement of the large woman in turquoise pants who owned both the hair salon next door and the car dealership, the crowd groaned at every vehicle. None of them were deemed worthy of the great Prester Mack no matter how often the woman pointed out excellent features—like having four tires and a working radio—with the hair scissors that were still in her hand.

Charlie had watched his stepfather, curious. He knew Mack well enough to know that he would be fine just fitting in. But no one wanted him to fit in. He was the great hometown success story returned—they wanted to see his success, to feel it more closely than when he had just been Prester Mack running around on the TV, playing ball thousands of miles away.

Every man in the crowd had tried to sell Mack some relative's car. They had argued with the hairdresser, but carefully while those scissors were open.

Finally, Mack had just called a luxury dealership all the way in Palm Beach. The crowd had cheered. The car was being delivered. The hairdresser had offered Charlie a trim. Charlie had ducked away.

Next was a visit to the realtor's, and the realtor had been in high school with Mack, and he had wanted to show them three perfect houses right away, but he had wanted to be Mack's long-lost best friend even more.

All three houses had been empty, yellow, overgrown, with yards that backed right up to a wall of cane. Charlie hadn't even looked at the broken barbecues or torn trampolines. He had stared at three different backyards that all edged another world. He had seen what could come from that cane. He had smelled what could come from that cane. And even in the sun, as those cane sticks shook their heads in the breeze, he had tried not to turn his back on them.

The realtor had ended by pitching houses in neighboring cities. Mack wasn't interested. The realtor said he had a friend with rental listings all the way in Fort Myers—beach houses, right on the sand. He'd make a call. Mack had laughed, but he hadn't argued. A rental might be good. Something comfortable. For a little while, until Charlie's mom adjusted.

They'd skipped lunch.

Mack's meetings at the school had been eternal. Charlie had been offered a brief secretarial tour, but he'd shrugged it off and gone wandering around on his own, staring through the glass in classroom doors. He'd been in the hall during one rush of bodies, and his out-of-placeness and the schoolness of it all had been too much for him. He'd finally fallen asleep in the library.

And now, football practice. Sun. Heat. Shouting. Drills. Boys much bigger and much faster than he was, making his stepfather yell and bellow and laugh in a way that Charlie never had.

He had found shade against the side of the small cinder block building that held two locker rooms along with the public restrooms. Hunger moaned inside him, but there wasn't anything he could do about that. Shutting his eyes helped. But only slightly. Open or shut, all he could see was Cotton standing at the motel room door, pumping his bike, running through the cane, crawling up the church hill in the moonlight, disappearing down that alley.

A long, sharp whistle jolted Charlie's eyes open.

The boys were all in the middle of the field, all on one knee, all with helmets off. And every head was turned toward Charlie—players, coaches, water boy, and even big Prester Mack, with his whistle in his mouth and a ball on his hip. Mack flipped the ball to a boy in the front of the crowd. Charlie recognized him as the boy caught the ball and jumped to his feet—white, skinny, slick black hair. At the gas station, his jacket had been labeled SUGAR.

Sugar turned. He cocked the football back with a long, lazy arm, and then he threw it.

Charlie could catch. He could run routes and dive for balls. He had done exactly that hundreds of times in the front yard while Mack chattered instructions and challenges, roaring like a crowd whenever Charlie made the catch, or mocking Charlie like a sportscaster when he failed.

But this was different. This ball was coming from more than forty yards away. This ball was coming in like a rocket. This ball was coming in while an entire high school football team and dozens of scattered observers were all waiting to see if Mack's boy—if Bobby Reynolds's boy—could catch.

Charlie hopped up, slipped on the grass, and slammed his back against the wall. His first instinct was to cover his head and dive out of the way. In one burst of motion, Charlie pushed off the wall, stepped forward in a crouch, and then jumped. He stretched his arms above his head, straining to snag the nose of the tightly spinning ball.

He had jumped too soon. Charlie began to drop just as the ball reached him. It folded back his fingers and sprang up into the air. Charlie leaned backward, grabbing at nothing, watching his failure spin away behind him.

He landed on his back in the grass and his breath exploded out of him. His eyes were on the sky. The ball hopped on the corner of the locker room roof and bounced back off. Charlie kicked himself toward it. He stretched out one arm and felt the ball slap against his palm.

It rolled off into the grass.

Groans washed across the field from the players and laughter trickled out of the stands. He shut his eyes.

"Charlie Boy!" The voice was Mack's. "Get on over here!"

Charlie didn't want to. He didn't want to get on over anywhere. He wanted the grass to eat him, to erase him from this scene completely.

"Charlie!"

Ignoring Mack was going to make it worse. Charlie rolled over and stood. He snatched that stupid ball up from a little nest of grass and jogged onto the field toward his stepfather.

The players were all stripping off their shoulder pads and dropping them onto their helmets. Sugar shot Charlie a smile.

"Nice effort, Charlie," Mack said, and he held out his hands for the ball. Charlie tossed it to him hard and tight—harder than he needed to. Mack caught it and laughed.

Mack pointed away across the field, over the top of the cane, toward the swamp. Brown sugar smoke rose up in a jagged tower, slow and stiff at the base, torn and feathered by wind hundreds of feet up. Behind the smoke, gray clouds on the horizon were hatching a change in weather.

"Time we ran some rabbits!" Mack said.

A few boys whooped. A few boys groaned.

Sugar crossed his arms. The sleeves were missing from his sweat-soaked shirt. His arms were purple and green with old bruises above the elbows.

"Seriously, Coach?" he asked. "Rabbits? I mean, I know you're old school, but that's kid and tourist stuff now."

"Tourists? In Taper?" Mack laughed, tucked the football on his hip, and walked toward Sugar. Charlie could see sparks growing in his stepfather's eyes. His voice was part drumbeat, part growl. "Old school? Son, it's as old school as going undefeated and wearing rings, old school as quickness and toughness and white stripes on grass."

Sugar worked hard to meet his coach's stare, but Charlie saw the boy's Adam's apple bobbing. Mack leaned his face close and let his words roll.

"Now, I know my team captain isn't standing here whining like a pussycat at a granny's back door. What is it you need, son? A little scratch behind the ears? Or would you like to win some games?"

Sugar said nothing.

Mack grinned and thumped Sugar on the shoulder.

"Nah. You're no pussycat. Wildcat, maybe. But when this coach tells you something, you don't open that gap-toothed mouth of yours unless a *yes, sir* or a *yes, coach* is hopping out."

Sugar nodded. Mack turned back to the whole team. "Time I saw some speed, boys! And, you know, my wallet's a little heavy. Think you all could lighten it for me?"

"Yes, sir!" the boys shouted.

"I've got a five for every muck rabbit," Mack said. "A twenty for any cottontail. Practice is over when the team has snagged ten."

Charlie watched the boys laugh and yell and bounce while Mack formed them up in two lines and sent them jogging away toward the smoke.

Mack faced Charlie. "Sorry about that ball. I thought you were watching."

Charlie shrugged. The crowd was trickling away. Assistants were collecting balls.

"You want to get out in the cane and run some rabbits?" Mack asked.

Charlie looked at the rising smoke. At the cane. At the

63

pack of boys jogging toward it. He wanted to know more about the muck and the fields. About what was out there. He wouldn't be alone. And the sun was up and shining. But he still felt his chest tightening at the idea.

"Are you coming?" Charlie asked.

"Prester Mack!"

Mack and Charlie both turned. A fat man in a yellow polo shirt stood beside a brand-new silver Range Rover parked on the grass next to the field. He held up car keys and jingled them.

"New car," Mack said. He glanced toward the smoke. "Awful timing. I'll have to sign something." He pointed after the running players. "Catch up to them. You're doing this, too, Charlie Boy. Go! I won't be far behind you."

While Charlie watched, Mack clapped his hands and jogged toward his new car. Stragglers who had been watching practice now drifted toward the silver beauty. It shone like lake water in moonlight—like a lure.

Charlie turned away from it. And he ran.

✳ ✳ ✳

There were trucks in the smoking field. And huge machines with faces like monstrous steel insects, grinding up acres of sugar stalks with the leaves all burned off. Charlie was moving down a long dirt road beside a deep canal. Overhead, charred leaves fluttered through the air, slowly turning to brown feather ash. Beside him, the machines chewed through patches of cane still crackling with flame—blades whirling and slicing, mandibles gnawing, filling huge bellies with diced sugar knuckles, spewing piles of sweet smoking segments into the backs of dump trucks that were slow-roll-floating over the soft dark muck on huge balloon tires.

Charlie slowed to a stop, transfixed by the total annihilation of the field beside him. Everywhere that he had seen a peaceful tower of smoke quietly climbing the sky, this onslaught had been going on below.

The roar of the harvesters was enormous, but a long, sharp whistle still found Charlie's ears. He turned. Sugar was standing on another dirt road across the canal behind him. The lean quarterback pointed at a little stone and culvert bridge fifty yards farther up. Then he turned and loped away.

✳ ✳ ✳

Charlie found the boys crouching in a long line in a shallow ditch between two fields. The black dirt was bare and loose on both sides of the ditch, and it swallowed his feet like soft sand as he crossed.

Sugar had taken his place near the center. Charlie stopped at the end, beside a boy with a baby face on a body the size and shape of someone's front door.

Most of the boys had stripped off their cleats. Some had stripped off their shirts and tied them over their faces like outlaws.

"I'm Surge," the big boy said to Charlie. He shifted slightly away, making room.

"Hey." Charlie nodded and crouched down beside him. "I'm Charlie. What now?"

"Take off your shoes if you don't want to lose 'em. They gonna light it soon. Then things is gonna be crazy."

"Why do they burn it?" Charlie asked.

"Fastest way to strip the leaves," Surge said. "Stalks is so wet, they don't burn."

A heavy white farm truck turned into the field beside Charlie. The driver looked out his window at the boys, and, for a moment, he looked concerned. Then he laughed and shook his head. The truck bed held a large gas tank, and a gun that looked like a water cannon was mounted on top, pointed to the side. A small pilot flame flickered beneath the barrel mouth.

"Here bunny, bunny!" someone shouted. The line of boys laughed.

"We downwind," Surge said. "They light the sides and it burns our way. Every living thing comes our way."

"Everything," Charlie said. His eardrums were thumping with his heart. This was it. He had stepped into one of Mack's party stories, and he wasn't at all sure that he was ready.

66

"Smoke, snakes, rats, and rabbits," Surge said. "But mostly smoke."

The white truck eased itself into position between the canal and the crop. And then heavy, wet flame burst out of the barrel and into the wall of ripe cane, every stick of it clothed in dry brown leaves.

Spewing fire, the truck bounced forward.

At first, there was only a little smoke. Crackling. But the fire moved inward, into acres of dry and eager fuel. The wind pushed it toward the line of boys.

Heat slammed into Charlie like a breaking wave. Beside him, Surge pulled his shirt up over his mouth and nose. Charlie did the same.

The crackling became a growl, and the growl became a sucking roar. Sugar knuckles popped like gunshots. Brown smoke rolled across the ground; it rose and raced away through neighboring armies of cane. It swallowed boys. It climbed the sky and cut off the sun.

Charlie's eyes streamed. A long black leaf with fiery edges grazed his cheek and broke on his shoulder.

Through the smoke he could see red tongues rising up taller than houses, snapping like circus tents in a storm.

Boys were whooping. Surge lumbered forward.

Charlie pressed his hand against his shirt mask and squinted at the black ground in front of the cane. Two rats raced out and veered toward the canal. Something much faster darted out—the first rabbit. Surge lunged and the rabbit veered away, back down the line of boys. A human shadow jumped after it. Hunched-over human shadows were darting everywhere.

"Possum!" someone whooped.

Charlie heard a snarl and Surge yelled in surprise. A large shape rose over the ditch and then a hissing bobcat landed beside him. Fur kissed Charlie's leg, and then the cat was gone.

The smoke was narrowing as the burn moved toward the center of the field. Charlie saw daylight and crawled toward it, ash tears dripping from his nose. A boy jumped over him, laughing. Another shape swore and dropped to the ground, rolling in the hot muck, slapping out a small fire on his shirt. Charlie rose to his feet and staggered away, just another living thing trying to escape the burn. And then a rabbit landed in the muck in front of him.

It was big. Its tail was cotton white. Without even thinking, Charlie grabbed at it. He missed. Muck flew and a foot thumped against his fingers as the animal reversed direction and exploded away.

Charlie was already running after it, back into the smoke.

Shapes flashed in front of him. He ducked under a tall boy's arm. He slammed into someone's back. Twice the rabbit reversed almost into Charlie's arms. Twice it danced back into the burning field and reemerged like a rocket.

Twice it drew other hunters, and then shook them off onto easier prey. But it didn't shake Charlie.

Flames were pouring out the side of the field now—licking the muck, smoothing ash over silty earth with fiery fingers.

Charlie hardly noticed. He was chasing, reacting, exploding after the animal. He was quick. His heart was pounding, his chest was tight, his breath was gone, and the soil pulled at his feet like deep sand. His legs and lungs were burning more than his eyes when he staggered out into the sun.

The rabbit leapt off the edge of the canal in front of him, landed in the still water, and began to swim. The field across the canal was now bare down to the black earth. Vultures swirled above it, looking for the remains of all that had been slow. Two huge harvesters with steel mantis jaws sat idling in the cane rubble, waiting for the next burn to clear the leaves.

Charlie staggered toward the canal after the rabbit, but a hand grabbed his arm and turned him around.

"You crazy, coz," Cotton said. He tugged Charlie's shirt down off his face, grinned, and pointed at the water. Ten yards away from the rabbit a small gator was gargling back a rat.

"Non compos mentis," Cotton added. "I like that one. Now, let's git."

Charlie blinked and shook his head, trying to focus. "Where?" Charlie asked. He snorted, spat, dragged his forearm across his nose, and spat again. "Where were you?"

"Doing what needed to be done," Cotton said. "Seeing what needed to be seen. Now we really gotta git. No lie, coz." He pointed again, this time through the gentle ash blizzard, down the long dirt road beside the canal. The sheriff's car was coming, trailing dust onto Mack's new silver car behind it.

Sugar jogged into the road and tugged his own mask down before leaning his hands on his knees. He watched the wet cottontail climb out of the water and bound up the opposite bank.

"Hey," Charlie said.

Sugar looked up.

"Tell my dad I found Cotton. Tell him I'll see him back at the motel."

"Your dad?" Sugar sneered. "I'm not telling *him* nothing."

"I mean Mack," Charlie said. "Tell Mack."

He left the quarterback coughing in the road.

✳ ✳ ✳

A man stood on the deck of his idling harvester. He had long hair the color of mud, a nose that had been broken more than once, and a blurry blue tattoo of a buccaneer on the back of his hand. A cigarette burned between two thick oil-stained fingers.

He had forgotten to smoke. For the moment, he had even forgotten to breathe.

He watched the two boys race down the road until they turned and disappeared between fields.

One boy, he didn't know.

The other had been his son.

THE LION'S DIRGE

Mack stepped out of his new car and squinted around. The field beside him had almost burned out. Brown smoke had become gray, and the wind was already stripping it away. Shafts of naked, bony cane stood in shadowy rows, ash below and smoke above. He knew what it would feel like to duck into that graveyard, he knew the heat the cane would press into his palm if he gripped a stalk. He knew the smell of the small, smoking bodies he would be sure to find back in ash shadows if he went searching.

He looked up. Dozens of vultures swirled around the thinning base of the pillar of smoke. Those birds knew it, too. Creatures of the cane were quick, but sometimes flame was quicker. When the harvesters had rolled, the vultures and crows would do their searching.

Mack turned toward the heavy machines waiting

across the canal just as one of the drivers ducked back into his cab.

Sheriff Spitz and Deputy Hydrant were both already out of their own vehicle and adjusting their belts.

"Hey, kid!" Spitz shouted at Sugar. "Charlie Reynolds make it back out of the smoke?"

Sugar looked straight past the sheriff at Mack. "Charlie just took off. Said he found that kid and he'll see you later on."

"Did he now?" The sheriff turned and eyed Mack over his glasses. "He saw something, Prester! You knows it and we knows it, and that's that. There's animal blood all over the church, a tree smashed right through a coffin in the bottom of an empty grave, and the bent-up bicycle of a missing boy—a boy your Charlie was with last night and says he's with again. Someone's going swamp-cat crazy, and no mistake."

"No mistake," Hydrant said.

Sugar's mouth was open. His eyes bounced from the cops to his coach.

"What coffin?" Sugar asked. "Whose grave?"

Mack watched the vultures. He watched smoke sliding away. Mack had known Charlie needed to talk, but he'd assumed he was just nervous about the new school, or worried about Cotton.

A grave robbery? Who would want to steal a dead

football coach? *Why* would they want to steal a dead football coach?

Why would they want to paint blood on a church?

There were no nice answers in his head. Whatever was going on, it was far from friendly.

"He take off alone?" Mack asked. No one answered. He focused on Sugar. "Charlie. He take off alone?"

Sugar shook his head. "No, sir. Like I said, he was with that skinny little homeschool kid. *Rat* or *Fluff,* or whatever he's called."

"Cotton?" Mack asked.

Sugar nodded. "Quick kid."

"And Charlie said he'd see me later?"

Another nod from Sugar. "At the motel."

Sweating, coughing, ash-dusted boys were straggling out of the field toward the cars. A few held small brown rabbits by the scruff while they kicked in the air.

Surge, grinning, cradled three thumping rabbits against his stomach with one arm. A hissing possum dangled by the tail from his other hand.

"Sheriff," Mack said. "I'm sure I'll see you later. Right now, I have some debts to settle. At least your missing-boy case is closed." He pulled out his wallet and walked toward his players.

"Not sure it is," Spitz said. He jerked his sun visor down into place. "He's still missing, ain't he? Maybe he's my body snatcher. Weird enough kid."

"Oh," Hydrant said. He shook his head slowly and held up his right hand. "He weird all right. 'Bout bit off my pinkie finger few months back. Weird."

Mack didn't answer. As he handed out bills, rabbits were released at his feet—hopping over his shoes and even hiding under his car. But he didn't notice. His mind was elsewhere, searching for Charlie, trying to see whatever it was Charlie was seeing, whatever it was Charlie had already seen.

The harvesters shifted into gear and rumbled forward.

❋　❋　❋

Charlie jogged along behind Cotton. The pace wasn't hard, but his lungs still felt the heat of the burn, and smoke residue tickling at his throat made him want to double over and hack.

Cotton turned down another long dirt road beside yet another long, deep canal. Charlie turned after him and saw two gators slide quickly under the water.

"You hear about the church?" Cotton asked. He slowed and came even with Charlie.

Charlie sniffed and licked his lips with a dry tongue. He could manage a couple words between pounding strides.

"We were there."

"No," Cotton said. His breath was easy and even. But he hadn't been in the smoke. Or maybe he had. "After. Big blood-map painted on the church. Cops think it's

75

craziness, but I know it's a map. And a tree. Ironwood tree planted in Coach's grave. That part *is* craziness."

"How do you—" Charlie said.

"Know it's a map?" Cotton finished. "'Cause I read."

"Map of what?" Charlie got the question out before hacking.

"The mounds," said Cotton. "I recognized the shapes from a book." Cotton turned around and began running backward beside Charlie. "Last night, I went back for my bike. It was bent-up, so I just left it. That grave-robbing resurrection man was gone, couldn't smell no stink monster anywhere, but blood was up on that white church in all those circles and crescents and lines and craziness and I was pretty sure I'd seen it before, and I even knew where I had. So I went and busted into the library."

"What?" Charlie asked. He had been slowly accelerating, trying to get Cotton to turn back around.

Cotton grinned, turned, and fell into step beside Charlie.

"Break in all the time. Little purple building with a flat roof and a busted latch skylight just my size. Looks like a gas station outside but nice enough inside. Sleep there sometimes."

"Why?"

"Coz," Cotton laughed. "If you were running away from a stack of books, where you figure no one would ever look?"

Charlie smiled despite his burning lungs.

"Secret is," Cotton said, "I ain't never running from piles of books. I run from the books she be putting in the piles." His eyebrows went up. "You ever hear of the Brontës?"

Charlie shook his head.

"Well, don't," Cotton said. "Ever." Cotton slowed to a walk and then paused, getting his bearings. Charlie leaned over his knees.

Beyond his own breathing, he could hear . . . nothing. The fields were quiet. Looking back, he could see the smoke and distant circling birds. Forward, the scruff of swamp trees was just visible over the cane.

Cotton picked his path, and Charlie followed, this time walking. After a few hundred yards, they reached a narrow canal between the cane and the trees. The trees were anything but quiet—birds squalled, mammals chattered, bugs clacked and pulsed. But when Cotton spoke, he whispered.

"Watch my back, coz. Don't want nothing coming up behind." Bending over at the waist, Cotton moved forward along the canal, his eyes locked on the shadows between the dense trees on the other side.

Charlie hurried after him, constantly glancing back, watching the tight wall of cane slide past.

Away from the burn and no longer running, he could feel the air cooling. A breeze was blowing, swaying the cane and rustling the green hair of the swamp trees.

They passed a dirt road between fields, and as they did, Charlie glimpsed the white church away on its mound. A cop car sat beside it. For a moment, the silhouettes of three men stood out against the sky before disappearing behind the cane as Charlie kept moving.

Cotton was leading them back to where that crazy old man with the sword and helmet, Lio, had first stepped out of the swamp, where a dead snake had been curled on a pale stone.

As they climbed onto the low mound and turned to bridge the canal, Cotton froze. Behind him, Charlie stopped breathing.

The white chalky stone was hidden beneath the curling bloody body of a large panther.

"Is it dead?" Charlie whispered.

Cotton inched forward. "On the stone, they're always dead."

Both boys waited. They stared at the motionless shoulders, at the back of the limp neck. The cat was big—bigger than either boy—and the fur was tan where it wasn't matted nearly black with blood. One ear was missing, but the other was backed with night-dark fur. The tail, thick and kinked like an old abused hose, had a tip as black as wet muck.

Charlie's mind spun. Was this one of the panthers from last night, the panthers that had chased the shadow away from the graveyard? Had the shadow killed it?

Cotton was a statue. After a long moment, Charlie slid past him. He crouched down and crept within reach of the body. He extended his hand like a doctor, to feel for a pulse.

The body was still warm. Fur as soft as a kitten's slid between his knuckles. Fur scabbed rough like bark scratched his palm. Fur sticky with fresh blood clung to his fingertips. The soft thump of a dying heart shivered just beneath the loose skin of its neck.

The kinked tail rose slowly and then slapped the ground. The one ear twitched. The ribs heaved in a long, wet rattling breath.

Charlie swallowed a yell and tried not to move. The heartbeat fluttered again beneath his fingers. Behind him, he heard branches swing as Cotton slid away.

The panther heard it, too. The huge cat's neck twisted slowly beneath Charlie's hand. Eyes like two golden moons poured light into Charlie's. The body tensed. Black glass pupils sharpened and the panther's lip quivered and curled, baring white teeth, inches long.

Charlie jerked back his hand, slipped, and sat down. But the big cat's eyes had already lost their focus. The animal's head hit the ground while its ribs heaved in quick, shallow bursts.

"Charlie!" Cotton hissed. "Get out of there! C'mon!"

Charlie shifted onto his knees. He could feel the heat coming off the cat's body, and smell the sour odor of blood mixed with the scent of decaying meat on the animal's breath.

Charlie gently placed his hand on the cat's belly and felt the sputtering breaths. He ran his hand up the cat's thick ribs and found the broken beat of the animal's heart. And that's where his hand was when the drumming of life finally stopped.

"It's dead," Charlie said. He glanced back at his cousin. Cotton was crouching on the far side of the canal with one hand over his mouth.

"What do we do now?" Cotton asked.

Together the boys managed to lift the panther off of the white chalk stone and shuffle across the mound and into the swamp. Cotton led the way, guiding the cat and Charlie over logs and around trees, toward the row of small collapsing shacks that he'd pointed out to Charlie at their first meeting.

Charlie had his arms hooked beneath the cat's front legs, its large head lolling against his stomach, tracing swirls of red onto his shirt. When they reached the most intact of the shacks, Cotton turned his back to the cock-eyed door, and the two pallbearers pushed inside.

In the light that filtered between the boards of the tiny half-collapsing space, Charlie could see rows and rows of buckets and jars and jagged halved soda cans lining the walls, all of them full of bones—full of the dead collected from the white stone and entombed by his cousin.

Together the boys lowered the panther to the ground.

"Biggest thing to ever die on the stone," Cotton said. "Do you think it could be this cat's blood on the church? I heard the cops say it wasn't human blood. Or maybe the Stanks killed the other one, too."

"Stanks?" Charlie asked. "I just saw one."

"Me too," Cotton said. "But there were footprints all around my bike when I went back. Three bare feet and one shoe. I've heard stories about Stanks in the deep swamps, Charlie, and there's never just one. Crazy Carl who sleeps in the street says there's a whole haunted tribe back in there. I always thought that was just campfire spook, but not anymore. Of course, the stories aren't all true. Even Crazy Carl says the Stanks stay out of the cane. And that's obviously wrong."

"A haunted tribe?" Charlie shook his head. "I don't believe it."

"Whatever they are," Cotton said, "I don't think they much care what you believe."

Cotton raised his hands over the panther's body like a minister, but he didn't seem quite sure what to say. Charlie knew it involved dust and ashes, but he couldn't remember the order.

"Into the valley of the shadow of death," Cotton finally said, "rode the six hundred."

"What?" Charlie asked.

"It's from a poem," said Cotton. "And six hundred

people live in Taper." He shivered and stepped over the panther toward the door. "I need the light to show you this."

Charlie followed Cotton out of the shack and over to a fallen tree covered with moss, where he tugged a packet of papers out of his waistband and began unfolding it.

"Map," Cotton said. He dug a broken pencil out of his pocket and circled a spot for Charlie. "You are here," he said.

Charlie stared at the paper. Black ink lines on white. The edges and creases of the paper were yellowed with age. The swamp was represented by zigzags. The cane wasn't marked at all, but there were more than a few canals, all labeled. But the real point of the map was the mounds. They had been traced in slow curves through the swamp, ending in solid circles or squares, running straight through what could only be cane and even dead-ending against a curved line labeled *Lake O*. The church was on the map, right on a mound circle. The town of Taper was nowhere to be seen.

A row of holes dotted one unfolded seam.

"You tore this out of a book," Charlie said.

Cotton shrugged. "No one had checked it out in thirty years."

"Except you?"

"Including me. I just borrowed it some. Doesn't matter. Point is all these mound lines were painted onto the side of the church. Some others, too, that aren't on here. But right where we're standing—where that white death stone is—well, on the church wall it's marked with a circle. It's not on this map."

"Okay . . . ," Charlie said.

Cotton looked at him. "And there were other circles just like them. More death stones, probably. I didn't count them. But at least two way, way back in the swamp. And even one"—he tapped the emptiness on the map, labeled as the lake—"out here."

"In the water?"

"Maybe water," Cotton said. "Maybe not. This map is older than the dike. It's not just water on the other side. Some of the wildest swamp is over there—places so thick only a snake could get through."

Cotton tapped the map. "I'm telling you, coz, the death stones matter. Don't know why, but they do. Stanks know they do or they wouldn't have slapped them on the church in blood."

"But why paint the map on a church?" Charlie asked.

"Thugs and punks always tag things," Cotton said. "Maybe the Stanks were marking turf . . . or marking what they want to be their turf. Could be the mounds and everything used to be theirs and they want it back."

"Stanks . . . ," Charlie said, testing the name.

"They are called Gren."

Charlie and Cotton both jumped. Lio stood only fifteen

83

feet away from them. His helmet was on and his sword was in his belt. He scratched slowly at the tight, curly scruff on his neck. In the daylight, Charlie could see patches of white in his beard, clustered along his jaw.

"And what they want," Lio said. "*Tout bagay.* Which is to say: everything. You. Me. The wind. But first, all that the mounds touch. The Gren are slaves to a Belly the mounds feed, and that Belly can never be filled. It sleeps. It wakes. It is devouring."

"What do you mean?" Charlie asked. "What Belly?"

"Hold on," Cotton said. "First tell us why you stole Coach. You've been pretty freaky yourself."

"William Wisdom was my father, and he would have been defiled. I have honored him even as you have honored my fallen lion—removing him from a place that was wrong and giving him to peace. I thank you. His mate thanks you."

"Panther, actually," Cotton said. "And you're welcome. But why should we trust a crazy grave robber in a helmet?"

"Why should I trust you?" Lio asked. "Boy liar and book thief."

Cotton shrugged. "Do or don't, I don't care."

"Nor I," Lio said. He smiled.

"Fine," Cotton said. "We'll be leaving."

"I trust you," Charlie said. "Mack saw you once. You saved his brother from a snakebite."

Lio took one step forward and stared at Charlie with wide, unblinking eyes. Charlie wanted to look away, but he knew he shouldn't. Finally, the man spoke.

"And I give trust to you. You are my brother, born of trouble."

Cotton shook his head. "Charlie—"

"What happened to the panther?" Charlie asked.

Lio sighed, then clenched his right fist and touched it to his chest. His face was solemn. "Gren happened. As Wisdom grew ill, Gren grew strong. When Wisdom died, Gren sought his body for the Mother's evil. Under old moons, Gren fled from my cats like prey. Under this moon, he stood strong. My great one, my lion, is *mouri*—is dead."

Charlie shifted his weight on the soft ground. The panther, the mounds, the foul shadow, the dead coach, the strange man in front of him, all of them were sliding around in his head like pieces in a puzzle that wouldn't quite click together. There was a picture here, and he could almost see it. He wouldn't stop looking until he did. Cotton was restless beside him, scanning the trees.

"Where's the other panther?" Cotton asked.

Lio pointed up. Ten feet above them, the big, sleek cat was crouching on a branch—ears forward, eyes locked down on the boys, black-tipped tail swaying slowly beneath the branch.

Charlie didn't move. He stared into the wide living

eyes, beautiful and certain like his mother's. They had clearly already made sense of him, and he was no enemy.

"That shadow, the smell, the Gren, what is it really?" Charlie asked.

"He is the mouth, the jaw, the fangs—Gren is he who chews and swallows. He is made of man," Lio said. "But when the mounds wake and the stars pull, he is much more than man. And much less."

Thick air moved. The paper map lifted and slid along the log. Cotton jumped forward and grabbed it.

Lio's nostrils widened and he pulled in the moving air. Then he hissed between his teeth.

"*Desann.*"

The panther dropped out of the tree, landed lightly on the log in front of Charlie, and then leapt toward Lio. Her tail brushed Charlie's arm as she went.

"I am not strong here," Lio said. "I will tell you more where the land is free."

"Let me guess," Cotton said. "Over the dike?"

Lio nodded and moved quickly toward the shack that had become a bone house. At the doorway he dropped to his knees, and his panther sat beside him. While the boys watched, Lio began humming slowly, and then he raised his head and sang. The words were unknown to Charlie's mind, but not to his bones. A shiver swept across his skin and sadness tightened his throat. Lio's voice matched the trees and the breeze, it matched the cat beside him and the old sword in his belt, his song was the sunlight sliding between high branches and the shadow he cast when it found him.

When he stopped, the panther beside him raised her head and yowled, long and slow. Then Lio touched his head, both shoulders, and his chest. He stood.

"We go," he said. "And quickly. The Gren is not far."

SEVEN
OVER THE DIKE

Lio didn't run, but his strides were long and quick. Behind him, Charlie and Cotton walked, then jogged, then walked again, struggling to match his pace toward the lake and its tall dike.

In front of them, the panther loped along easily, her shoulders swaying, her tail swinging. At least until Lio hissed a command and she darted ahead, or doubled back and ran behind, or slipped into the cane on one side or the other.

"Could have cut closer to the church," Cotton said. "Faster."

Lio ignored him. The panther shot ahead and then paused, waiting.

"Where did you get the sword and helmet?" Charlie asked.

"I am Lio. I did not *get* them. They were given."

"Okay," Charlie said. "So who gave them to you?"

No answer.

"What did you mean the Gren is made of man?" Charlie asked.

"Flesh of man," Lio said. "Soul of all that muck rots and mounds gather."

"Smell of skunk," Cotton said.

"Can you kill him?" Charlie asked.

"I have killed the Gren many times," said Lio. "When he is weak and young. But when he is ancient and strong, he fells me."

"I don't know what kind of roots you've been chewin'," Cotton said, "but you should stop. You're not even making half sense."

"I am only the Lio of now. Not the Lio of then. There have been many."

Cotton laughed. "And lots of Stanks, too?"

Lio looked back over his shoulder and stopped. "The Gren is many, but all of one soul and one Mother. Many devils, but one hunger, one hate. One Gren."

The air had continued to cool and the breeze had become a wind. As the cane walls swayed and rattled around them, Lio dropped into a crouch and scooped up two handfuls of soft, silty black muck.

"All places have *lespir.*" He pressed the two handfuls together and let the dark earth trickle slowly between his fingers. "*Soul. Spirit.* The words are well but not perfect

89

truth. You see the darkness of this earth? It is rich, men say."

He focused on Charlie, deep eyes almost hidden in the shadow beneath his helmet. "Rich with death. With life made silent, pooled, sleeping, and waiting to rush into any vessel—green cane, the iron tree, two boys. A dead man made *diab*—a devil. So many lives, where the many waters brought them, laid them down, and made them black earth. Every creature now breathing beneath the sun could fly from flesh and sleep in these earth beds, and the muck would grow no darker."

He brushed off his hands and stood. "Trees feed on slaves and kings. Cane rises up from forests and flocks and peoples. Where so much death is, life waits, and there is much power."

Lio inhaled slowly and leaned his head back, eyes closed, feeling the wind. The panther had disappeared while he was talking.

Charlie shivered. He wanted to laugh and pretend like none of this could be real. Dead men? Life from the muck? But he had smelled that awful taint, and the sick memory of it was even in his bones. He looked at his cousin. Cotton's eyebrows were as high as he could make them, and he'd sucked his chin in toward his neck.

"You're fighting Stanks over the muck?" Cotton asked. His lip twitched up at the corner.

Lio raised his hands above his head, growing taller as

he did. "Long ago, when men believed such things, when they searched for powers to awaken and serve, they found this place. Beneath the stars, they built their mounds. Priests woke and named the rich death in the muck. They died and walked again. They laid down love and took up hate. They became Gren."

Not far away, hidden in the cane, the panther screamed.

Charlie jumped and yelled before he even knew what he'd heard. Cotton spun around, knees bent, ready to run, but not sure in which direction. Lio drew his rusty sword and turned slowly, pointing the notched and bent blade at the cane on both sides. He glanced up at the sun—it was low enough to paint cloud crowns with flame, not low enough to reach their bellies.

"Gren have left the trees," Lio whispered. "Beneath the sun's fire."

"I don't smell anything," Cotton said. "We'd smell him, right?"

Lio turned his back to the breeze and pointed downwind. Cane swayed and rustled on both sides of them, bending in the same direction, pointing with their bent green blades.

"*Kouri*," Lio said. "Go. Run. *Kraze dike e koule.*"

"What?" Charlie began to back away, trying to see in every direction at once. Something could be invisible in the cane just five feet from him.

Cotton was cocked and waiting to spring, like a

frightened bird ready to fly. "No Creole," Cotton said. "No Creole, no Creole, no Creole!"

"Over the dike," Lio said. "Down the dike, feet on the chalk stone. Straight out to the great tree—*straight out!* Through swamp and water. The great tree and no other. Go now. Run!"

Off to the left, the panther screamed and cane clattered. Lio turned toward the noise. Behind him, the cane exploded. A huge shape with long human arms slammed into Lio's back and rolled him to the ground.

Cotton grabbed Charlie's sleeve, jerking him away from the two snarling bodies and the horrible smell, dragging him into a run.

Charlie's legs should have been tired. He'd run much and eaten little. Smoke still scratched the insides of his throat and lungs. But something deeper was moving his legs now, something ancient and simple and stronger than stars. He was quick, not dead. Time was irrelevant as his legs chewed up the muck, as they strained and bit and spat, as the wind split around his face. He felt as fast as falling rain, his steps a spatter of heavy drops hitting almost at once.

Cotton was beside and behind him—Charlie could hear his breathing, he could see the blur of his knees and feet. Together, they were flying between walls of swaying cane. They were alive.

And then Charlie looked back. And in that moment, he didn't feel fast at all.

The dark shape racing behind them was faster. It wore a slashed panther's head like a hood, and bloody panther skin flapped and snapped behind it like a cape as it ran.

Charlie yelled. There were no words, but Cotton understood and surged forward. They reached an intersection between fields and Cotton turned hard. Charlie slipped, grabbed at the ground with both hands, and just barely kept his feet. Yelling, he put his head down and sprang forward, digging with frantic feet like he was trying to turn the whole world beneath him.

Ahead, Cotton's strides were short but furious.

Charlie heard chuffing behind him. Heavy feet were punching the earth. He wanted to scream. He wanted to cover his head, fall to the ground, and vanish. His heart was beating against spikes of terror. He was the rabbit. And he knew he was caught.

Pain.

Something hard and sharp swiped Charlie's right ankle. He felt his right leg swing behind his left. Shin slammed into calf. Charlie rose, floating, his legs spinning to the side, his head and shoulders dropping to the other. He threw up his arms and felt his elbows drag through the muck. His head was where his feet should have been. And he wasn't done spinning.

Muck flew. The ground folded and flipped him—knee to jaw, knee to cheek, teeth to tongue. As Charlie tumbled to a stop, his nose filled with stench, and anger erupted through the pain. He hated the world. He wanted it smashed. Every sunny day. Every laugh. Every father. Shatter it all even if he was shattered with it.

And then he saw Molly in his mind. The stench would take even her.

"No." Charlie spat the word into the dirt. He saw Mack and his mother. "No," he said again.

Two hot hands grabbed the sides of his face from above. They twisted hard, rolling him onto his back.

Charlie kicked against bony legs. He grabbed at the hands on his face and felt his nails break. He gagged on mud and blood draining into his throat, all while staring into hard blue eyes and a young man's face painted with cracking mud, looking down at him from beneath a bloody rotting hood of panther skin.

"Stank!"

A rock hit the man in the shoulder and bounced away.

"Leave my cousin alone! Let him go!"

The Stank looked up. Another rock floated past, but this time too high.

The Stank opened his mouth and his upper lip curled, baring overly large, overly white teeth. Charlie thought he was snarling, but the lip curled too far, too high. The man was actually smiling.

"Cotton, go!" Charlie shouted. He twisted and kicked, but the Stank didn't even glance down.

"Shut up, coz!" Cotton said. "I'm not going anywhere till this freak is gone."

The Stank ducked as the next rock caught him in the side of the head. When he looked back up, his eyes were angry. They looked into Charlie's. One large hand moved to Charlie's throat. The other picked up the rock Cotton had thrown. It raised the rock high.

Charlie's head felt like a blood balloon ready to burst. His blurring eyes focused on the gray stone instead of on the man holding it. Cotton was shouting.

The big arm dropped.

A sleek panther caught the mud-caked wrist in her teeth. Her body slammed into the Stank's, and the two tumbled off of Charlie.

Cotton was still shouting, but now he was also dragging Charlie through deep, soft soil. He was pulling Charlie to his feet. He was pushing Charlie, shoving Charlie, trying to make Charlie run down the narrow lane between the fields.

Charlie's ears were ringing. His eyes wouldn't focus.

His right ankle was all fire.

"Ow," Charlie said. He couldn't even hear himself.

Cotton was tugging at his wrists. Cotton was trying to run.

"Ow!" Charlie yelled. Still nothing.

The fire in his ankle was spreading up his calf toward his knee. Somehow, he was jogging. And then running—but not straight. He veered toward one wall of tall green sticks and then back toward another. There were many green sticks on both sides, and he didn't know why, and he didn't have time to stop and find out, because he was running. And the more he ran, the more the flames inside his leg spread through the rest of him, and the more the stench faded behind him.

He didn't know how they made it to the hill. It was a big hill, almost a wall. The other boy was trying to make him climb it.

"No," Charlie said, and he knew the other boy heard him, because he stopped and looked angry and afraid. He couldn't remember the other boy's name. Charlie shut his eyes and went looking for thoughts in the darkness inside his skull. He found one and opened his eyes.

"René," Charlie said.

The boy stopped yelling. Shiny tear stripes lined his dark cheeks.

"René," Charlie said again. "Don't cry. It's French for *girl*." He'd heard that somewhere. He smiled and blinked slowly.

The boy punched Charlie in the face. Charlie staggered backward and fell down. The boy stood over him, but he was looking around, not down at Charlie.

"René," Charlie said. "French for *stupid*. Fact."

* * *

Cotton looked down at his stupid white step-second cousin. Charlie was a mess. His right leg was swelling up nice and fat beneath the knee. His tongue was bleeding, his leg was bleeding, and now his nose was bleeding.

They were halfway up the dike. The sun was almost beneath the clouds and dropping fast. Friendly panther or not, Cotton was not going back into those fields in the dark. Not with that . . . Gren anywhere near.

Charlie smiled. "René," Charlie said. "French for *stupid*. Fact."

Cotton punched his cousin again. Hard enough to hurt his own hand. He shook it loose while Charlie fell back in the grass, unconscious and gargling. He might feel bad later, but this was easier right now.

Plus, people who called him that got punched. Minimum.

Cotton grabbed Charlie by the ankles and backed his way up the dike as quickly as his cousin's weight would let him. At the top, he dropped into the grass beside Charlie, breathing harder than he had when running from the Gren.

Flat on his back, arms thrown wide, Charlie opened his eyes. Above him, the falling sun was burning its own fields. Dark clouds sailed over the dike on fiery bellies.

Charlie's leg felt as heavy and thick as a log. He could

97

smell traces of the Gren's rot still on him. He could smell fermenting flowers somewhere nearby. The breeze traced cool trails across his face and arms, carrying hints of salt, which could only mean *sea*.

Staring at the sky, Charlie felt like he was still floating, like he still hadn't landed since his legs had been swept out from under him. Above the clouds, where the sky was marching from blue to night, he could see pricks of light— whispers that marked worlds, suns, and galaxies. As he stared, they grew brighter and bigger. They filled the blue and burned through the clouds and scattered sparks when they collided with sunlight at the bottom.

Charlie's stomach turned and he shut his eyes hard. Something inside him knew he couldn't trust what he was seeing. He was sick. Or hurt. Or both.

"Charlie," Cotton whispered. "Charlie, you have to get up. I can't drag you anymore."

Charlie squinted. Cotton was on his belly beside him. He looked frightened.

"We have to go, coz. Can't stay here."

Charlie nodded. He held his breath and rolled onto his side. His leg screamed, but he fought his way up onto his hands and knees.

"Good," Cotton said. "Stay low, and follow me."

Charlie looked back over his shoulder at the cane fields that stretched away from the base of the dike. A dark shape in a panther cape stood motionless at the edge of a field.

"Cotton . . . ," Charlie said.

Cotton swore. Charlie threw his arm around Cotton's shoulders, and together they limped across the top of the dike. Charlie saw no lake. He saw veins of dark water—tangled pools reflecting sky that disappeared beneath shaggy trees, and a canal like a moat that lined the base of the dike. The lake trees stretched away as far as Charlie could see.

Staggering down the inside of the dike, Charlie slipped in yellow flowers. He tumbled and rolled, pulling Cotton after him. He didn't remember standing back up, but he must have, because he was limping again, leaning on Cotton. They crossed an overgrown path. They slid over a thick rusty pipe. They reached the canal bank of jagged gray boulders packed with white shells.

"There!" Cotton said, and he pointed across the canal. "The great tree. That cypress."

Charlie could see its scraggly head rising up above the others from somewhere back in the lake swamp, but he couldn't remember why that mattered.

Cotton was dragging him along the bank, staring at the ground as they went.

"Chalk stone," Cotton muttered. "Chalk stone, chalk stone, chalk stone."

Charlie looked back at the dike as a black shape rose above it. And then a second shape appeared beside it. Charlie blinked. Two of them. Like tombstones in the sky.

"Stanks," Charlie said.

"Get on!" Cotton slid in front of Charlie, bent his knees, and looped Charlie's arms around his shoulders. He levered Charlie up onto his back, and then he tried to run. Charlie's feet dragged and bounced through grass and over rocks as Cotton grunted and groaned beneath him.

Above them, the two tombstones dropped out of the sky and broke into a run. Their legs were long.

"No!" Cotton shouted. "No, no, no!"

Bones crunched beneath Cotton's feet. Bones were everywhere, small and bleached and broken, spread in a wide halo around a smooth chalky stone in the grass.

"Hey," Charlie said.

Cotton slid on the death stone, nearly dropped Charlie, and then faced the water. He stepped out onto the boulders on the bank, wobbling, rocking. Charlie saw a snake dart away.

He heard snarling behind him.

"Swim, coz!" Cotton screamed, and then jumped into the brown water. Charlie slid away from his cousin. Kicking one leg and dragging the burning one behind him, he flailed both arms, pulling himself through liquid.

Hands were sure to close on his ankles. Heavy bodies were going to crush him from above.

Charlie pulled harder, and the water cooled around him. It was getting deeper. He let himself drift on the surface. He filled his lungs and looked back at the bank. Cotton was doing the same. They were almost across the canal.

Both Stanks stood on the grass just shy of the death stone. One was much taller and broader than the other. While Charlie watched, the tall one bent down and snatched a fat snake from the rocks. He raised a long arm, bare of everything but caked mud, and held the snake up in the air. Over and over, the snake struck his arm, but he didn't so much as flinch. Finally, he closed his fist around the biting snake's head and squeezed. Then the big Gren laid the dead but still writhing snake on the white stone.

Cotton spat out a mouthful of water. "It was them," he said. "On the stone. All those animals, all these months."

On the bank, the smaller Gren pulled a long bone knife out of his belt and raised his arm to throw.

The blade flew.

EIGHT
MOTHER WISDOM

Charlie dreamed.

In his dream, an alligator ate his leg.

In his dream, Molly wore a rotting panther skin and chased him around, laughing.

In his dream, an old woman kissed him on the head and sang to him. She sang about love. She sang about running. About wind. About heroes and beauties and spicy rice. She sang about chains breaking and seas rising up to kiss the sun. But mostly, she sang about sleep. And when she did, he slept. And when he slept in his dream, he dreamed a new dream.

In his new dream, he ran barefoot on a dirt path between fields of cane. The dirt was a strange powder of forests, of fish, of birds, of men and women and children and wolves, of huge reptiles, and of mushrooms. It swirled beneath him as he ran, and every grain sparked into white flame when he touched it, and the flames swirled up in a cloud behind him, and he laughed, because he knew Molly would laugh and because he felt like a comet. His flaming tail was made of life, and every spark told a story about every living thing that had ever been and every living thing that would ever be.

Charlie laughed from the sheer joy of it, and he ran faster. His tail of sparks grew into a tornado, a hurricane, a galaxy of living dust, and still he ran.

He looked back at the cloud of life behind him and saw it rising up from the cane higher and brighter than any field fire and its smoke. But also in the cloud, there was a writhing shape. It had many limbs and wings and heads and hates. It was as black as nowhere and as empty as never, and it was swallowing the cloud of sparks. A long arm of dark emptiness lashed out and whipped itself around Charlie's ankle.

Pain. Terror.

In his dream, Charlie would scream.

In his dream, the old woman would kiss him on the head and sing a different song, not about sleep. She would sing her song about spicy rice. Or the moon. Or a river. Or a tree with roots so deep that they grew straight through the whole world and became a forest on the other side.

* * *

Charlie yawned. He could hear the rain. It sounded like there was a big puddle just outside his window. Molly would be happy. She would jump in the puddle in her bare feet because feet were meant to be in puddles and toes had been invented so that mud could squirt between them.

"Molly . . . ," Charlie said. He sat up in bed and looked out his window.

Except there was no window. There wasn't even a wall. He was on a low cot beneath an old green blanket. The cot was on an uneven plank deck suspended between two massive tree trunks. Above him, thick living branches grew out of one tree and into the other, belonging to both trees equally. Beyond the deck and the roof, there were more trees, all of them rising up out of black water that was puckered and rippling with raindrops.

Charlie kicked off his blanket and swung his feet over the side of his cot. His right leg throbbed, but the pain wasn't sharp. He wasn't sure what had happened. Something about Cotton throwing rocks. Had Cotton hit him?

Charlie pulled his knee up to his chest and twisted to get a look at his ankle. His shoes and socks were gone, and a large square of sticky gauze covered the source of his pain. He peeled it off. A rough gash at least three inches long and one inch wide decorated the outside of his ankle. Thin lips of white flesh shone where it had been torn open.

The wound wasn't bloody at all. It was packed full of busy, glistening maggots.

Charlie shut his eyes hard and swallowed, his throat tightening. He was waiting for something, something that would change what he had just seen, that would carry it all away and make it disappear.

Slowly, his mind crawled out of its sleep shell, and he knew that he had been waiting for the old woman and her kiss and a song. He was waiting for the dream to change.

But this was no dream.

Charlie opened his eyes and leaned slowly over his ankle. The wound was real. The maggots in the wound were very real. He wanted to shout and jump and shake them off. Instead, he shivered. Someone had put them there on purpose. And as disgusting as they were, they seemed tidy. He carefully pressed the gauze back down over those little wriggling gray backs. He shivered again at their squishiness, and then lowered his foot back to the floor. The pain grew as he stood. Everything from the knee down hummed.

Engravings swirled across the dark planks of the floor. Animals—panthers and gators and rabbits and birds. Snakes. Boys running. Charlie recognized the church carved on its mound. Canals. Even a few odd little buildings and streets that had to represent Taper. And there was a cane field burning—flames carved like looping waves. In the cane, crudely engraved men hacked with machetes. Crudely engraved women carried bundles of cane on their backs toward wagons waiting on a road. A man on a horse swung a whip.

Against the bottoms of his bare feet, the engravings felt like pinecones, or barnacles on a rock.

On the ceiling, the planks had been carved with moons, suns, and stars. Paths had been traced between the moons, connecting them all. The same was true of the suns and the stars. There were so many lines it was impossible to follow a single thread. Around the edges, strange creatures had been carved as well—three eyes clustered together between spread wings, a lion with hooves and wings and a roaring man's bearded head.

"Honey," a woman said behind him. "What are you doing up?"

Charlie spun around and winced, lifting his injured foot and balancing awkwardly on his left leg.

The woman had white hair pulled back into a loose single braid. Her eyes were blue, and her skin was pale beneath a thick spray of dark freckles. She was thin but not bony. Her shirt was square and loose and a shade of white that approached yellow. Everything about her was soft—everything but her eyes.

"You were in my dreams," Charlie said. "Singing."

The woman smiled and nodded.

"I didn't recognize you then," Charlie said. "But you were at the coach's funeral. Beside the grave in a white chair. The man, the coach, was he . . ."

"He was," the woman said. Her smile grew. "I've been Mrs. Willie Wisdom for fifty-nine years, and just because he died doesn't mean I have to stop. The boys called me Mother Wisdom." She winked at Charlie. "Prester and his brother called me Mama Molly."

Molly. Charlie wasn't sure what to say. He lowered his right foot and eased his weight back onto it. He pointed at his ankle.

"Did you, uh . . ."

"I did," she said. "Some poisons are beyond doctors."

"Poison?" Charlie asked. When could there have been poison? He remembered being chased, but it all blended together with his dreams. Sparks of life swirling around him, and then brutal pain erupting in his ankle.

"Mrs. Wisdom, where's Cotton? How long have I been here?"

Molly Wisdom took Charlie by the hand. She led him past the empty cot to the other open wall. More trees. More rain. And two flights of covered stairs that curled away behind the huge trees. On the right, the stairs went up. Mrs. Wisdom went left, to stairs that descended.

She took each step first, holding Charlie's hand, supporting him with her soft shoulder as he limped behind. The stairs were just long enough to wrap around to a lower room on the other side of the tree. This room had trees on two sides, one wall open to the swamp, and one that connected to a narrow footbridge that seemed to run from tree to tree above the water. There was a soft rug on the little room's floor, a bookshelf, a dresser, a cupboard, a small bed, and two red chairs with worn but bulging cushions. Quiet embers glowed in a metal bowl on the open side of the room, and a bright blue teakettle hung on a hook above it. A few raindrops reached the kettle and the fire bowl and hissed themselves dry on impact.

Mrs. Wisdom helped Charlie to the nearest chair and then bustled over to the teapot. Charlie watched her pull heavy stone mugs from the cupboard. He watched her pack herbs into a little metal strainer above the mugs and then trickle steaming water through the leaves into the mugs. Finally, she pressed one heavy mug into Charlie's hands and then nestled herself into the other chair, pulling her feet up onto the cushion beneath her. She held her mug with two hands, inhaled the steam, and then smiled.

"So, Charlie Reynolds, I suppose you'll be wanting to know everything."

Charlie nodded. "Yes, ma'am." He looked down at his mug. It felt like a large hot rock. The rim was almost too thick for drinking. The liquid—tea, he assumed—was the color of caramel.

"Double honey and cream and a little extra something for that infection of yours, doll," Mrs. Wisdom said. "Do try it. Now, you learned some things in your dreams, but I never know how much sticks. So, how about you tell me what you'd like to know first."

Charlie watched Mrs. Wisdom watching him as she

sipped her tea. He licked his lips and then looked at the rain.

"Where am I?"

Mrs. Wisdom laughed. "Why, you're right here with me."

Charlie shifted in his chair, frustrated. Mrs. Wisdom leaned forward and held up one hand.

"Don't be squirming, honey. I know what you meant, and I'm sorry for making light. You're in a swamp grove that once stretched strong all the way to Old Nick Slough, not too far from Moonshine Bay, in the shallow western waters of Lake Okeechobee herself. If it weren't for the dike named after the lovely Mr. Herbert Hoover, you could see the lights of Taper glowing from the tops of these very trees. My dear departed Willie trained and built this part of the tree house, and Lio helped him. Most of the rest was trained and made by those who came before."

Charlie raised his mug and decided against it. He let it rest on his leg, and then moved it quickly to the soft threadbare arm of the chair.

"Where's Cotton?"

Mrs. Wisdom nodded. "You're a good boy, Charlie Reynolds. You must be wondering all sorts of things right about now, but worrying about your friend comes first. And it should. Cottonmouth Mack is asleep. Across the bridge with all the others."

"The others?" Charlie asked. "What others?"

"Sixteen of them," Mrs. Wisdom said. "Poor little dolls. Four more than Willie and I ever had to care for out here, but sadly fewer than actually needed my help."

"I don't really understand," Charlie said. "You're saying that Cotton's okay?"

"He is," Mrs. Wisdom said, but her voice grew heavy. "As okay as any of us are right now, and to be honest, that isn't very okay at all. He could be dead by midnight. As could you be. As could every poor soul in the sweet little town of Taper, Florida." She dragged her fingernails across the arm of her chair. "We're outmatched, Charlie Reynolds. All places and peoples have their ends, just as much as they have their beginnings. I'm just one more selfish old woman who doesn't want the sun to set just yet." She smiled with tight lips, and her blue eyes were wet. "You've seen the mounds. The weak chalk stones. The Gren. Your eyes have seen the life magic in the muck."

"All the dust that turned into sparks?" Charlie asked. "That was a dream. I'm not really made of fiery dust."

"Yes," Mrs. Wisdom said, "you are. You're made of tiny spinning bits as fast as light. But those bits aren't all of you. They fly off. They get lost, and new ones come on and join the swirling Charlie-shaped dance that is your body. And dwelling in that dance, woven through every racing bit, heating it all with life and guiding it, there is a fire, a soul—*you*. It takes a dream to see something like that, something closer to the way things really are."

Charlie stared at the old woman. He'd listened in science class. What she was saying wasn't really all that different from how Mr. Kahn had talked about atoms and electrons and all that stuff. Even the look in their eyes was the same—bright and wild, like they were talking about magic. Because they were.

"Charlie?" Mrs. Wisdom asked. "Are you okay?"

Charlie stared down at his untasted tea. "In my dreams, the muck was all fiery, too. But it's dead." He looked up.

Mrs. Wisdom turned and pointed at the embers in her fire bowl. "The muck is like those coals. Quiet, still, full to overflowing, waiting to erupt back into the dance of life. Millions of lives from millions of different kinds of living things have formed our black soil. Putting a seed in that ground is like throwing paper onto my coals. But plant an evil seed . . ."

Mrs. Wisdom's voice trailed off. She rose from her chair, walked to the fire bowl, and stood beside it, looking out between the trees at the rain and the water.

"Charlie, honey, come here."

Charlie limped over to her. Rain dribbled off of the roof. Spatters reached his toes and hissed quietly on the lip of the fire bowl beside him.

"The Gren are not alive with their own fire," Mrs. Wisdom said. "They are human seeds made into vessels for an evil as old as Cain, and the mounds were used to feed them. Long ago, the Seminole pushed the Gren back into

111

the swamps and set twelve stones into the mounds to cut their power and cage the evil. Now only three stones remain. Two protect water. One protects the fields around Taper. Lionel tends it, but with my husband gone, he cannot hold it long."

"The one by the church?" Charlie asked.

"Yes," said Mrs. Wisdom. "And if that one is broken, the mounds will feed again, the Gren will grow, and Taper will be empty within the month."

"Empty . . . ," Charlie said.

"Burned. Dead," said Mrs. Wisdom. "Devoured. If Lionel had not saved the body of my Willie, it would be done already. The stone would have been shattered and my Willie would be one of the Gren. But he's safe now, even if we are not." She pointed straight down at the water. Charlie watched the drops pucker the surface. He watched slow rings grow and collide with each other, and then his eyes focused beyond the surface. A long stone box sat in the tree roots on the bottom, its lid looking almost within reach. Even through the rippling distortion, Charlie could see two letters carved side by side on the lid.

W W

"So much life in my Mr. Wisdom." Mrs. Wisdom dabbed her eyes, laughed, and then slid her arm around Charlie's shoulders and pulled him into a soft hug. "Do you mind, doll?" she asked. "I'm sorry, if an old lady needs a hug, she takes a hug." She retreated back to her chair. "Now drink that tea and tell me what else you want to know."

Charlie's eyes were still focused underwater. Beyond the old coach's box, there was another, and another—ghostly rectangles hiding under the rippling surface.

Mrs. Wisdom nodded. "Every graveyard for miles around is empty of its dead. The Gren would take them to a grove where their mother plants bodies and harvests muck-born sons. My Willie stole them first and gave them peace in the water. Water keeps them out of reach."

"I want to go home," Charlie suddenly said. "Please."

"Home," said Mrs. Wisdom. "Soon, love. But not just yet."

Charlie turned around. "Why not?"

Mrs. Wisdom nodded at the mug in Charlie's hands. "It'll be cold now, honey."

Charlie raised his mug and gulped the entire drink down. It wasn't cold at all. It was hot and sweet and nearly scorched his throat. When he'd finished, there was a heat in his gut so heavy he felt like he'd swallowed the mug itself. He exhaled and was almost surprised not to see steam.

"Why not?" he asked again. "How long have I been here?"

"Three days," Mrs. Wisdom said. Her blue eyes grew heavy. "You can't go home, doll, because this is the only place in the world where you are still alive."

MAGGOTS AND TEA

Natalie Mack paced in front of a wall of glass. One arm hugged a ragged gray sweatshirt to her chest. Her other hand pulled at a row of absurdly large championship rings hanging on a simple silver chain around her neck. She fingered through them like beads as she walked along beside the huge floor-to-ceiling windows in the beach house Mack had rented. She knew why she was holding Charlie's sweatshirt. She wasn't sure why she had put on Mack's rings. Because she wanted to trust him?

No game he had ever played mattered as much as what he was trying to do right now.

Outside the glass, rain was attacking an uncovered pool and pelting scattered deck chairs. Beyond the pool, palm trees swayed and bent in the wind like ferns on fishing poles. Beyond them, the Gulf of Mexico thumped on sand.

Natalie forced her pacing feet to stop. She couldn't stop her pacing mind.

One hour. A lot less given how she would be driving. That's how far away she was if the call came. And it would come. Mack would call. He would hand Charlie the phone. She would hear her son's voice and then she would load Molly into the car and they would fly through the rain.

Even as she thought it, she knew it wouldn't happen that way. If Charlie was fine, Mack would bring him to her. Taper wasn't safe right now. It was like the whole town had unhinged all at once. Every old grudge had blossomed into a feud. Every old feud had exploded into violence. She couldn't be there with Molly. Her first two nights had proved that completely. She'd heard the gunfire and seen two buildings burning from their motel room. While Molly had slept, she'd stood looking out at the midnight fires. And she had seen *him*—Bobby Reynolds, Charlie's father—sitting on the hood of his truck beneath a street-light, ignoring the flaming chaos only a block behind him, staring at the motel from beneath a battered trucker cap. Smoking.

Natalie had snapped the curtains shut, gathered Molly up in a blanket, carried her daughter into the bathroom, and locked the door. Her fingers had been shaking when she had called Mack. Bobby had been gone by the time Mack had arrived.

After that, she had been willing to move to the beach.

How things could get so crazy in such a small town, Natalie had no idea. And Charlie was stuck in it. Somewhere.

Natalie turned away from the window. Behind her, Molly had pulled a shaggy white faux-fur rug onto one of the three white leather couches and nestled in on her back. She had a small plastic zebra in one hand. Her other hand was empty, but it was still managing to carry on a conversation with the zebra. They were talking about Charlie. All three of them—the hand, the zebra, and Molly—were in agreement. If Charlie were here, *he* would sneak out with them to play in the rain and everything would be better.

Natalie crossed the room and slipped onto the shaggy not-fur beside her daughter. Her arms slid around small ribs and squeezed. She pressed her face into her daughter's hair. She inhaled life. She wanted to count every breath, every quick beat of Molly's heart that she could feel against the inside of her arm. She wanted to thank that little muscle for every single one of those small thumps.

Molly and her hand and her zebra chatted happily, ignoring the grown-up and her very wet face.

Natalie's phone rang.

❋   ❋   ❋

"I don't understand," Charlie said.

"You're alive," Mrs. Wisdom said. "Here. But only here, among my trees. If you left, the farther away you got from them, the more that Gren poison in your leg would grow, the hotter your fever would burn, until . . ." She grimaced. "You *were* dead when I found you. Cotton had managed to get you to the first of my trees even with that awful knife through his shoulder. He had one arm around you and one arm hooked over a cypress root, poor love. He died shortly after."

Charlie's feet stopped. Mrs. Wisdom tugged on his arm, but he didn't budge. Cotton? Dead? Knife? Charlie remembered being in the water. He remembered Cotton coming to help him. And then he saw it, the Stank drawing that long bone knife and raising his arm to throw.

"He's breathing now," Mrs. Wisdom said. "But not well. C'mon, honey. I'll take you to him."

The narrow bridge was slick with rain. Charlie's eyes were on the water as they walked, watching pale stone coffins ripple and warp beneath the surface.

"The great trees drink of the deepest muck magic," Mrs. Wisdom said as she walked. "They drink, are filled, and overflow. Just breathing their air does wonders. Many times, I nursed my Willie's wounds in this place, as my mother nursed my father's. By the end, when Willie's old heart finally stopped, he had so much swamp life stored up inside, it practically erupted out of him. Lio said a tree sprang up in his grave overnight. Did you see it?"

Charlie shook his head.

"Well, I'm glad it did," Mrs. Wisdom said. She led Charlie around the base of another large tree. A floating dock bobbed at its base. A strange canoe was tied to it. The boat had been hollowed out from a single log. It was long and sleek, and waxy smooth even where blade tracks textured its sides.

"Lionel carved that canoe for Willie," Mrs. Wisdom said. "It isn't the easiest thing to pull two drowning boys into, but that boat and an old woman did the trick. And it's quicker and quieter in here among the great trees than anything with a motor."

Mrs. Wisdom steered Charlie up another curling flight of stairs that wrapped around the trunk of a massive cypress tree. At the top, she stepped aside and gestured for Charlie to go first. He limped into a room bigger than his old school's cafeteria. The walls were railed instead of completely open. Three long tables formed a U in the center of the room around a large fire pit full of ash-seething embers. On the other side of the tables, more than a dozen cots were arranged in rows.

Above the fire pit, hanging from two hooks, was a severed arm. It was large—crudely torn off at the shoulder—gray, and muscled. The fingers were contorted. A hooked bone spike, sharp and pointed like a giant talon, was strapped to the back of the wrist.

"Welcome to my heriot," Mrs. Wisdom said. "Complete with a Grendel's arm, as distasteful as it is. Once, when I was your little Molly's age, courageous men and women laughed and feasted here. Now . . ." She sighed. "You ever read *Beowulf,* love?"

Charlie stared at the arm's painfully bent fingers, at the naked sinews jutting out of the shoulder. He shook his head.

"Cotton probably has," Charlie said. "Why do you have that arm?"

"Charlie, honey, that is the weapon and the arm of the Gren that struck you three days ago. Without it, I could not begin to stem the poison it planted in your flesh. The darkness that lashed your ankle would even now be swallowing up the last sparks of your fire."

Charlie shivered. The gash in his right ankle felt suddenly very . . . *open.*

"But how?" He looked at Mrs. Wisdom. "Who?"

She smiled slightly. "Bless Lio for his courage and his blade." She walked between the tables and stopped at the edge of the fire pit, sniffed in the arm's direction, and then turned back around. "The stench of every Gren is a little different, just as their soul rot is a little different. The Gren feel only hate and envy and rage—every other part of their human souls has been devoured. They are their own poison, and they are woven into everything they might care to make—most usually crude and cruel weapons. Their touch, even their stench with enough time, plants their particular curse in the soul—where no doctor could ever

119

see it. A wound from their hands is much, much worse. When they draw blood, the victim has very little time."

Charlie moved between the tables beside the old woman until heat rippled up against his face from the fire. Up close, the arm wasn't really gray, it was just coated with dirt, dried to dust above the fire.

"You still had the Gren's stink on you when I pulled you from the water. Lio's panther got the scent and tracked him. Poor soul. I'm glad I didn't see his face before Lio gave his body to the water. I prefer not to recognize them."

She nodded her white head at the arm. "Take it down for me, doll. It's not a trophy, and its usefulness has passed."

Mrs. Wisdom picked up a long bent cane off the table behind her and handed it to Charlie. When Charlie hesitated, she said, "It can't hurt you now, love. Every bit of danger has been washed and burned away."

Charlie took the bent cane, leaned out over the heat of the fire pit, and hooked the arm around the wrist, pulling it toward him. When it was close enough, he grabbed the hot forearm and handed the cane back to Mrs. Wisdom. He lifted.

The chains swung free above the fire pit. The hot, dry limb dropped into his arms. He swallowed hard and looked at the old woman.

"Hold no bitterness," Mrs. Wisdom said. "Forgive as you would like to be forgiven." Her clear eyes were full of pity, and she stared hard at Charlie, waiting for an answer.

He nodded.

"Good," Mrs. Wisdom said. "Now throw it in the fire."

A cloud of sparks swirled all the way up to the live beams in the ceiling when the arm hit the embers. Charlie was suddenly dizzy as he staggered back. Waves of dream memory pushed forward in his mind and for a moment the whole world seemed to be made of sparks. He slammed his eyes shut. When he opened them again, the sparks were gone.

Charlie turned, a little dizzy, and hurried after Mrs. Wisdom, supporting himself with the tables as he did. Cotton was at the end of a row of eight cots. An empty cot was beside him and then six boys Charlie didn't know, some big, some small, were stretched out sleeping on the others.

Cotton didn't look like he was sleeping. He looked dead and posed. His hands were crossed on his stomach. His legs were straight and tight together. His lips and eyelids were slightly parted. He was shirtless, and his skin, dark and bright and alive when Charlie had first met him, was now dull and dry and bloodless. He looked like he had been sculpted from clay. A gauze patch stuck to his chest above his heart.

"Is he breathing? Is he alive?" Charlie asked, his tongue as dry and stiff as an old shoe. "Why is he so much worse than me?"

"Breath enters him," Mrs. Wisdom said. "He is alive.

How long he might remain so is in Lio's hands now, and I fear even for him. He has been gone too long."

"Can't you stop the poison?" Charlie asked.

Mrs. Wisdom pointed to a wooden tray at the foot of the cot. A long bone knife lay in its center. The handle was heavy, but delicately carved with scales down to the butt, which had been shaped into a gaping, fanged mouth. The yellowing bone blade was long and sharp and viciously slender.

"No Gren carved that," Mrs. Wisdom said sadly. "They are raging brutes, all clubs and claws and teeth. Yours may have thrown it, but the poison was not his own."

"Then who?" Charlie asked.

"Their mother," said Mrs. Wisdom. "The one Lionel calls the Belly. The woman who births the muck-born."

"But Lio will get her?" Charlie asked. Panic skittered his heart. Fear was trying to melt his legs.

"Lionel is a selfless heart, a strong man without envy, but he was already twice wounded when he brought the arm of your Gren and set back out again to hunt the Mother." Mrs. Wisdom ran both of her hands across her freckled face and pressed back her white hair. "Even great men fall, love. And Lio has been gone two days."

Charlie wobbled on his feet. Breathing was becoming hard, and his eyes were blurring. This was more than fear, more than grief. This was . . . this was . . .

"Tea," he said. "What did I drink?"

The hall spun around him, and Mrs. Wisdom grabbed his hands.

"Sit," she said, lowering him into the empty cot beside Cotton. "This bed is for you. Sleep. Greet your cousin in his dreams before he passes."

Charlie fought to stand back up. "No!" He shook his head. "I have to go. Cotton needs help."

"Hush, love," Mrs. Wisdom said. "You need days more before you leave."

"Cotton," Charlie said. "Cotton . . ."

". . . is dying, honey," Mrs. Wisdom said. "Short of a miracle, he will be gone by midnight. But he is ready. His dreams are of peace. He is in the sun. He smells the sea. You will see him again when your own time comes, and the two of you will run together without fear, you will run on legs like wings made of joy and you will never grow weary."

Charlie's eyes closed. Gentle hands pushed him flat on his cot. His legs were straightened. His own hands were crossed. Sleep, warm and thick and wonderful, came to swallow him whole.

No.

No, no, no. He couldn't wake up with Cotton gone.

Charlie's eyelids felt like they had been sewn shut with rubber bands. He forced them open, straining to keep them from snapping closed again. Above him, tree branch beams blurred and fluttered like bats. *Stupid. Tea.*

He heard an engine. Voices. Someone somewhere was shouting.

Charlie tried to roll, and his own body was the heaviest thing that he had ever moved. Slowly, one shoulder rose off the cot. His legs crossed. He forced one leg farther and farther off the bed. He was on his side, on the very edge.

And then the cot flipped and Charlie hit the floor face-down. He lugged his arm out from underneath him and folded his limp fingers into his mouth, scraping his knuckles against his teeth. He had to get that tea out.

Charlie gagged. His stomach heaved. And then the rubber bands overpowered his eyelids and he was still.

Two hands grabbed his ankles. Pain, sharp and loud, screamed up his right leg. The hands dragged him out from between the beds and rolled him onto his back.

Fingers popped his eyelids back open.

Below the swimming ceiling, Charlie could see a smudgy Mrs. Wisdom. She looked upset. Crouching below her, holding Charlie's eyes open, was an older boy with hollow cheeks and very black hair.

"Sugar?" Charlie tried to say the name, but he only managed a gargle.

Blurry Sugar looked up at Smudgy Mrs. Wisdom.

"Wake him back up," he said. "Please! I need to talk to him."

Charlie's eyes slipped shut.

When Charlie woke, he was slouched forward on a

bench with his arms limp at his sides and his face dangling over a large wooden bowl full of thick, steaming green paste. A cloth was tented over his head, capturing all the steam along with an intensely fishy smell and pooling it into his lungs.

Charlie jerked upright, flipping the bowl across the table and into the still-smoldering fire pit. The soggy cloth clung to his head and cheeks, and the contents of his steam-cleaned sinuses clung to his chin. Sputtering, sneezing, he tore the cloth off his head, dragged it across his face, and threw it on the floor.

Whatever had been steaming in that bowl, he was now very, very awake. His feet were already bouncing under the table, and his eyes were so wide they hurt. Blinking, twitching, he scanned the room.

Sugar was sitting on the bench next to him.

Cotton was still on his cot. The empty cot next to him was up on its side.

Mrs. Wisdom was on the other side of the room with her back to the rail and both hands up on her freckled cheeks. Her sharp blue eyes were wide and worried.

Charlie pointed at her. "You! You shouldn't have done that!" He was shouting. He didn't mean to be shouting, but every cell in him was hot and full to exploding. His lungs felt like they could exhale for a week.

"Charlie . . ." Sugar slid down the bench toward him. "It's not that simple."

Charlie was still pointing. He pulled his finger in, but his fist was still out there. And it was shaking. He could feel his fingernails digging into his palm.

Sugar forced Charlie's hand down to the table. "Breathe, Charlie. Just sit for a minute. Let it settle."

"Why are you here?" Charlie shouted.

"Looking for you," said Sugar. "It wasn't easy. Mack and your mom are going crazy."

Charlie's body shivered long and slow, like a cold snake was climbing his back. His right leg kicked forward without asking permission. His fingers splayed. His mouth flew open and he began to yell.

And then it was gone. His body was his own again. His yell died. He was just Charlie, but with a complaining ankle and an open mouth.

Mrs. Wisdom dropped her hands from her face and breathed relief.

Charlie closed his mouth. After a moment, he pulled himself free of the bench and stood. His eyes went straight to Cotton, his cousin, the dying sleeper made of gray clay. Charlie had to do something. Anything.

"Things are crazy in Taper right now," Sugar was saying, "and the cops are useless, blaming everything on you and Cotton and anyone else they can think of."

"You have a boat?" Charlie asked.

"Yeah," Sugar said.

"Let's go," Charlie said.

Mrs. Wisdom stepped forward. "Honey, it's a brave thing to want, but it won't do any good, and it will do a whole lot of bad."

Charlie met Mrs. Wisdom's eyes. He wasn't angry at her. She'd saved his life. And Cotton's, too, even if only for a little while.

"How long do I have after I leave?" Charlie asked. "Before the poison takes over?"

"It all depends, love." Mrs. Wisdom looked years older as she answered. "The farther you go, the worse you'll feel, the less time you'll have."

"How long?" Charlie asked again.

Mrs. Wisdom shook her head. "I can't exactly say. If you leave, you'll find out for yourself the bad way."

"Tell me how to find the Mother," Charlie said. "And what to do. How do I save Cotton?"

"The Mother?" Sugar asked. He looked at Charlie, and then back at Mrs. Wisdom. "What are we talking about?"

"Charlie Reynolds," Mrs. Wisdom said. "Are you willing to die to save your friend?"

"He's my cousin," Charlie said, looking at Cotton. His throat was tightening. He raised his chin and exhaled slowly. "I'd rather die than not try."

Mrs. Wisdom nodded, sighing. "All right, love. It's your life to live and your life to give. But you'll be needing a few things."

TEN BRO

Charlie held a green waxed canvas bag on his lap. The bag had two shoulder straps and closed with a single flap and a loop that slipped over a wooden toggle. Two initials were embroidered on the flap in fraying thread.

W W

Charlie was sitting in the prow of a small square-nosed aluminum boat. Sugar was in the back, controlling a rusty outboard motor as he eased the boat past roots and trees.

Rain found them in sparse, heavy drops that slipped through the canopy above.

"Not too much farther," Sugar said. "Then it's open lake and we loop around."

Charlie didn't answer. He hunched forward over the bag, shut his eyes, and tried not to notice if he was already feeling worse. He was replaying Mrs. Wisdom's final words in his head.

Two little glass bottles.

"Two breaths of the *quebracho*—the ax-breaker. Iron-wood. Don't waste them, doll. Only when you're empty to the dregs and too dead to take another step. Those trees don't breathe but once or twice a century, and when they do, the puffs are strong enough to burst a man at the seams."

The bone knife that had wounded Cotton, wrapped in a cloth sleeve.

"Don't touch it till you have to, love. And pray it works on Gren flesh."

A green felt-tipped pen and Cotton's partial map of the mounds torn out of a library book. More mounds had been drawn onto it, copied off the church.

"Honey, the mounds are a true tangle, but they all lead to her grove in the end. She gathers her power through them. Just don't be getting yourself turned around."

A worn silver lighter.

"Deep water deals with Gren—washes the muck-birth right off of them. But burning is the only way for her. She's died a dozen times and it never stuck. Always the muck mounds refill her with life. If you get her down, light her up like cane. And throw that knife in her flames."

A tarnished wide-mouthed brass air horn, attached to a dented old can of air.

"Honey, those Gren've got no speech left of their own, so they hate noise like nothing else. That hate draws them."

Charlie inflated his cheeks and sat up. What on earth was he thinking?

I'd rather die than not try.

Seriously? Was that true? He had meant it when he said it. But only because Cotton had been lying right there looking dead. Because Cotton had saved him. If Charlie could be somewhere else and not know about any of this, if he'd never met Cotton . . .

But he did know. He had met Cotton, and Cotton had met him. When Mack had come, Charlie Reynolds had suddenly become more of a son than he had ever been before. When Molly had come, she had turned Charlie into a brother, adding deep loves and loyalties to who he was without asking his permission first.

Cotton had made Charlie a cousin. That could never be undone. And by tomorrow, Cotton would be alive or dead. And Charlie would have risked his own life for his cousin, or he wouldn't have. Which was just . . . nuts. It shouldn't be that way. He was only a kid.

"These creatures are made of envy, raw and ruthless," Mother Wisdom had told him. "Still, their greatest strength lies in *our* envy—their poison can grow that envy until it swallows you whole from the inside. But you're going as a giver, willing to give your life for another, and, honey, that brings its own protection. Picture Cotton with the gift you want to give him—a happy life—and even in the thickest stench, your mind might stay clear."

The rain had slowed and almost stopped. Accumulated drizzle dribbled down Charlie's neck and he shivered. Sugar was staring at him, but he looked quickly away from Charlie's eyes.

"How did you find that place?" Charlie asked.

Sugar swiveled the motor and slid the boat between a cluster of young trees.

"I got lost once," Sugar said. "I was only eleven. Jumped a cane train and couldn't find my way back. When it got dark, I went a little crazy. Saw things. Nightmare stuff. I don't remember much. I woke up a week and a half later in a hospital two towns away." He turned the boat slowly, winding through trees, and then grimaced when the rail thumped against a ragged stump. "From then on, I had all these tree house dreams. Mother Wisdom was in all of them, taking care of me and singing."

"And kissing your head," Charlie said.

Sugar laughed. "Yeah, well, two years later, I asked her about it. I told her what I'd dreamed."

"And she told you?" Charlie asked. "Just like that?"

"Mother Wisdom doesn't lie," Sugar said. "Not when she's asked straight up. I had a pretty good idea of where it was after that."

The trees around them were finally thinning. Charlie turned and got his first glimpse of Lake Okeechobee—

water, water, and more water. The lake had no edges but the sky itself, bending its back with the planet's curve, hiding its banks behind horizons.

Sugar turned the boat and throttled the engine all the way down. He let the little aluminum shell drift as they took in the view.

Charlie glanced back at him. "I know it's insane," he said, "but we should hurry. I haven't even gotten started until I get all the way to the swamp past the church."

Sugar burst out laughing. "Did you really think I was going to send you off on your secret swamp mission? No way. Everyone loves Mother Wisdom, but Mack is *Coach*. He would seriously kill me if I found you and then let you take off again."

Charlie's mouth fell open. For a moment, relief flooded through him, but it was just as suddenly gone. Charlie closed his mouth as Sugar throttled the engine back up and the boat surged forward through the drizzling rain and the fading daylight.

Bouncing in the bow, clutching his bag, Charlie was cold all the way from his wet skin to his shivering bones. Every time he blinked, he saw Cotton—made of clay, bloodless and still. He pictured another stone box sliding beneath dark water, one with coz carved on the top.

Eventually, the trees were gone, replaced with acres and acres of needle-tipped grass. The grass finally thinned and the boat slowed, turning into a narrow channel of water with green on both sides.

And Charlie was starting to feel sick. His head was lighter and his stomach was gurgling, threatening to knot. Pressure was building behind his eyebrows. His eyes felt hot, but the rest of him was cold.

Mrs. Wisdom had been right. Or maybe he was just boatsick. He hoped.

"We're south of Taper," Sugar said. "We'll double back up the canal by the dike."

As they entered the deep canal that lined the lake, Charlie scanned the dike. It was too tall for him to see anything behind it. Above it, he could see the distant aura of bright lights. Above the light, a helicopter was circling with a spotlight sweeping down from its belly.

"What's with all the light?" Charlie asked.

"Friday," Sugar said. "Football. First home game without Coach Wiz since I don't know when."

"Really?" Charlie asked. "Still?" He couldn't imagine people playing a game right now.

"Football and church," Sugar said, "don't cancel for nobody."

"The chopper?" Charlie asked. "Is it looking for us?"

"Nah," Sugar said. "Just for trouble. Town needs a game right now. Last couple days, people been hating in Taper like I've never seen. Craziness. Houses been broke into, diner got burned, every nice car in town been smashed up, muggings, two shootings. And the whole place keeps stinkin' up like skunk and sewer line."

"Envy," said Charlie. He wiped rain from his forehead and tried not to shiver.

"Rivalry game," Sugar said. "According to the cops."

"Mack's there?" Charlie asked. "At the lights?"

"Nah," said Sugar. "But someone there will know how to reach him. He hasn't stopped looking for you, not even to breathe." Sugar turned the boat and killed the motor. They were drifting sideways toward a dock in the shadow of the dike. Sugar stood up and stepped to the rail, leaning out over the water, stretching a long arm toward the dock. His throwing arm.

"Hold on," Charlie said suddenly. "What time does the game start? Why aren't you there?"

Sugar was silent. He pulled the boat up against the dock and held it while Charlie climbed out. Charlie watched him loop a rope around a dock cleat and then cinch it tight. The older boy dragged his arm across his forehead and sat back down. He picked up a stained and frayed ball cap from the bottom of the boat, pushed back his dark hair, and pulled it on. He didn't look at Charlie once through the whole process.

"What is it?" Charlie asked. "What's wrong?"

Sugar pulled his hat back off and stuck it on his knee.

He leaned forward, resting his head in his hands. When he spoke, it was to the bottom of the boat.

"I've hated you for a long time, Charlie. Probably as long as you've been alive."

Charlie blinked and took one step back.

Sugar finally looked up. "But now . . . well, now I don't."

"Why would you hate me?" Charlie asked. "We've never met before. I've never even been to this place."

Sugar exhaled long and slow. "Charlie . . . I'm your brother."

Charlie shook his head. "I don't—"

"Your dad, *our* dad, put a ring on my mom's finger when they were both in high school, before he left for college. They set a date. But then he hit the big time and was gone for good. She even bought a dress. When I was little, she would hang his football pictures in my room. When I was four, she took me to bars to watch his games on TV, bought me team gear from those fools who drafted him into the pros. Told me that my daddy was rich and famous and amazing." Sugar's voice dripped anger. He clenched his knees and rocked slowly where he sat.

Charlie was numb. He wiped drizzle from his eyes. Whispered through the distance, he could hear cheering. Drums. Chanting.

Sugar stared hard at Charlie.

"He never answered her letters. Never took her calls.

So my mom saved up money and then put me in a car, and we went looking for Bobby Reynolds. She still wore that stupid ring. We waited outside stadiums after games. I finally met him standing beside a team bus. He was surprised to see my mom. He looked terrified to see me. He told her never to come around again, that he'd gotten married. That he had his own son." Sugar laughed. "Looked right at me and said it. 'I have my own son.' I was five."

Sugar stood up in the rocking boat, smiled at Charlie, and shrugged. "So I hated you. For the next few years, I was birthday-wishing you dead so he would come back. My mom throws her ring in the swamp, burns her dress, moves us up the muck to Taper—where everyone already hated Bobby Reynolds—and then marries her fat old boss. Pretty soon after, Bobby Reynolds blows up hard and awful, goes to jail, and the next thing I know, I'm eleven years old and the word goes round that Bobby Reynolds is coming back to the muck. And even though he never calls and never comes by, I was just glad that you didn't have him anymore. You and me, we were finally even. Until I see a picture of you from the paper. People cut it out and stuck it up in just about every window in Taper. It's still under the glass by the cash register in the hardware store. Mack has his arm around your mom, and he's in his pads and he's covered with sweat and champagne and confetti, and he has you sitting up on his shoulder. And the caption says something simple like, 'Prester Mack celebrates with wife, Natalie, and son, Charlie.' I don't know how old you were. . . ."

"Eight," Charlie said, and he swallowed hard. He was feeling dizzy. And he was sweating, even in the cool, wet air. He could taste the salt on his lips. "Sugar, I—"

"I'm sorry, I shouldn't be telling you all this right now. It's just I've been sitting on it so long, and when you came to town, I was hoping for a chance." Sugar hopped up onto the dock. "It's not your fault. Coach Wiz got my head mostly straight when I hit high school, but when I saw you with Mack at the funeral, I was scared I might start hating you again. But I didn't. You were just . . . my little brother. I hadn't even thought about that part. I have a brother. That's why I'm not at the game. That's why I've been out looking for you."

"Sugar—" Charlie said. His ankle throbbed. His knee wobbled.

"Half brother." Sugar smiled. "I know. But out here . . ."

". . . brothers is brothers," Charlie finished. "I'm going to be sick."

For a split second, Sugar looked insulted. And then Charlie slipped onto his knees, flopped onto his belly, and threw up in the canal.

Charlie stared at the spatter on the water. He felt better empty and lying down. It kept the blood in his head.

But the water reeked. Even worse than his own chuck. Like sewage or something nastier. He snorted and spat and watched the dark ripples carry it away.

Sugar. His brother. He wondered if Mack knew. Why would he? It was strange and awkward and . . .

The smell was getting worse.

Why should Sugar hate him? Charlie was the one who'd gotten kicked around. Sugar was the lucky one. Of course Mack knew Sugar was his brother. He knew when he had Sugar throw that ball to Charlie. Mack had wanted to embarrass him, to show his older brother that Charlie was just an uncoordinated little tick.

Charlie blinked. That wasn't like Mack at all. He scrambled up to his knees. Sugar was standing above him with his hands on his hips. His lip was curling.

"You know, you reek." Sugar sneered. "Forget everything I just said. I should throw you into the canal right now. *Bro.*"

"No!" Charlie shook his head. He pointed past his brother. Sugar turned. A man stood twenty feet away on the narrow ramp between the dock and the bank. He was wearing a ragged cape of rotting raccoon skins, a pair of ripped-up pleated dress slacks, one shoe, and nothing else. A mass of mud ran up his torso and into his clumped and tangled beard.

Sugar took a step back. "Who are you?"

"Stank," Charlie said. He climbed to his feet. "He's one of the Stanks. Whatever bad things you're thinking right now, ignore them. It's the smell."

Sugar gagged. His eyes were hot with hate and his fists were balled.

Charlie was panting through his mouth, trying to ignore thoughts as quickly as they spattered across his mind.

The Gren pulled a massive hooked club over his shoulder and pointed it at the boys. But he didn't step onto the dock.

Why wasn't the Gren attacking?

"The water," Charlie said. "Mrs. Wiz said to get them into deep water."

✳ ✳ ✳

Mack eased out of his new car and stood in the open door with one arm on the roof. The headlights shone on a slumping, flat-roofed shack. A crumbling chimney decorated one end of the little building, and a cockeyed door was almost centered between two small windows. A light was on inside.

Mack's wipers squeaked across his windshield and went back to sleep. For just a moment, he shut his eyes and felt the rain. His stomach held nothing but coffee, and he needed sleep. His throat was raw from yelling in the cane and in the glades and at the sheriff. He'd almost gotten himself arrested.

He glanced into the backseat of the car. Natalie hadn't wanted to be in front. She hadn't wanted to be seen. She was leaning forward, peering through the windshield. Molly was asleep in the car seat beside her.

Natalie nodded. She was still wearing his heavy rings

around her neck. "This is it," she said. "He only brought me here once, but I'm sure."

Mack inhaled long and hard and stepped away from the car. A gun would be nice, tucked into the back of his waistband. Or some cops, though if they'd tagged along, they'd be more likely to arrest him than their old teammate, Bobby Reynolds.

All Mack had was a phone, his wife, and his daughter. And an awful feeling.

"Bobby!" Mack shouted. He walked toward the front door. "Bobby Reynolds!"

Mack stepped under a little stoop above the front door. He thumped the door with his fist, then tried the knob.

The cockeyed door swung open, dragging through a long, scraped-out groove as it did. Mack stared into the silent, glowing room.

"Bobby?" He stepped inside. "You here?"

There was a tightly made bed against one plank wall with a blanket folded at the foot. A lamp, a bookshelf, an overflowing ashtray. A thick rag rug, a woodstove, a sink, a refrigerator barely bigger than a five-gallon bucket, and a toilet sitting in a boxed-in closet with the door open.

Two newspaper photos hung on the wall, one of which Mack recognized immediately—Natalie had hung a large print of it in their bathroom. Mack was in his pads and drenched with champagne, holding Charlie on his shoulder. Natalie was standing beside him, laughing and lovely, more alive and beautiful than anyone he had ever seen. That part of the photo, worn and creased, was in Mack's wallet.

The other photo was of Sugar, his lean arms crossed, long black hair tucked behind his ears, and an almost-smile on his face. The headline above it read:

"SUGAR" TAKES THE REINS

That was it. No Charlie and no Bobby. Mack thumped his foot on the floor and looked down. A single piece of paper rested in the center of the rug. He picked it up.

Mack,
    Spitz said you might be coming. I ain't no monster. If I find Charlie, he'll be safe. Out looking for my boy, same as you (only he ain't yours).
                    Bobby

PS If you still want my blood after, then just you try and take it.

ELEVEN
THE LAST LIO

Charlie crouched at the very end of the dock with the bag under his arm and his hand inside, on the bone knife wrapped in cloth. If the Stank came at him, he could pull it out. He could fight. At least he wanted to look like he could.

Sugar was beside him. The tall Stank was still pointing his club. He hadn't taken one step onto the dock.

"What's he doing?" Sugar hissed. "That stink, it makes me . . . it makes me think . . ."

". . . awful things," Charlie finished. "Me too. Don't believe it. And keep breathing through your mouth."

Sugar groaned like he'd been punched in the stomach. Charlie felt the same wave of hate. He suddenly wanted to throttle his quarterback brother with the strong arm. He wanted to take that arm from him.

"No!" Charlie shouted, and the effort gave his mind

a small blast of clarity. "Change the subject. Think about something you know you love. Just . . . just run football plays in your head."

Sugar nodded, breathing hard, focusing on the still-motionless Gren. "What's he waiting for?" he asked.

"Us," Charlie whispered. "Probably doesn't want to risk being over deep water."

"Do you think he'll jump on me if I get in the boat?"

Charlie glanced at the boat, drifting where it was tied, then looked at his brother.

"Flare gun," Sugar whispered. "Or we just boat away?"

"He'd only follow us on the bank," Charlie whispered. "Grab the flare gun. I'll get him out here, then you shoot and knock him in."

Sugar nodded, then took one step and jumped into the boat. It bounced and splashed and swung out to the end of its rope.

The Stank tensed, crouching like a runner ready to explode. As Sugar rooted around under the seats, the Stank raised his club to throw.

"Hey!" Charlie shouted. The Stank turned to him, club still raised. Suddenly the crowd in the distant stadium erupted in cheers, the sound rolling down over the dike like a flood. Thousands of voices. Horns. Drums. Joy. The Stank snarled and rolled his neck and shoulders, writhing in pained irritation.

Mrs. Wisdom was right. The Stank hated sound.

"Touchdown," Sugar said from the boat. He held up a bright yellow flare gun.

Charlie fished around in his bag, found the heavy air horn, and pulled it out. He pointed it at the Gren.

"Where's your mother?" Charlie asked.

The Stank snarled.

Charlie shrugged and pulled the trigger.

The horn had been designed to signal distress across miles of water, to throw blaring sound beyond the horizon to the horizon that came after.

It did.

The blast shivered Charlie's teeth. The Gren screamed and fell backward onto the bank. But only for a moment. Even as Charlie released the trigger, the Gren was exploding forward onto the dock with his club raised. Two huge strides. Three . . .

The dock bounced under his weight. Charlie didn't even have time to jump.

A hot pink flare shrieked past Charlie, straight into the Gren's face. The flare careened off his forehead and corkscrewed up and away. The Stank slipped sideways and tumbled into the water, limbs flailing as he was swallowed in splash. A swirling mat of raccoon fur bubbled up in the wash.

Sugar jumped out of the boat to stand beside Charlie. As they stared at the roiling water, a man surfaced, no longer the terrifying creature that had fallen in. This man's beard was muddy but white and his bare back was moon-pale. The muck that had been caked on his shoulders had been washed away, and his skin was baggy on his bones.

The old man—for that was now all he was—flailed weakly toward the bank.

"Mr. Welles?" Sugar asked, but the man didn't answer. Sugar looked at Charlie, his eyes wide. "I knew him," he whispered. "He worked at the bank before it closed. He used to give me candy. Until he died."

Charlie didn't know what to say. He felt a little better now that the stink was drifting away, but he was still sweating, still dizzy. The old man in the water was struggling to pull himself up onto the boulders that lined the canal bank. His skin sagged off the ribs as he freed himself from the water. His movements were jerky. Clumsy. Dead. And then they stopped completely. The strange second life of Mr. Welles had ended.

Sugar was staring at the body.

Charlie looked around. One hundred yards down the dike, two more shapes rose in silhouette against the glow of the stadium lights. *The horn. And the flare.*

"We have to go," Charlie said. "Quick. To the swamps past the church, where the mound goes into the trees."

Sugar shook his head. "I told you. I can't let you—"

Charlie ran to the dike and began to climb. Sugar

caught up easily. When they reached the top, Sugar stayed low, practically crawling across the high, flat back of the dike to the other side. Charlie copied him.

Across the cane, Taper's lights were dull and yellow beside the humming white of the stadium. In the stadium, tiny boys ran into each other. Tiny people banged drums. The crowd stomped and chanted. The lights above the stands rocked slightly. The helicopter had moved on, but cop lights flashed in the parking lots and along streets. On the northern side of town, alone in the darkness, a single light glowed next to the white church on its mound.

Charlie wiped sweat from his eyes and squinted. It looked like a LEGO block from here. Or half a sugar cube.

The good news was that heading north through town to the church wouldn't take him any farther from Mrs. Wisdom's trees than he had already gone. Unfortunately, there was no way to know exactly when he would run out of time—Cotton's, or his own.

In the cane field below them, a small fire was burning.

"The flare," Sugar said. "Let's go." He turned sideways and began to run down the dike toward the stadium. Charlie followed. Or he tried to. His ankle groaned, and his legs were growing heavy—too heavy to listen to him. He slipped and slid and ran again. He slipped and almost screamed when his ankle scraped across a jagged stone.

Sugar was waiting on a dirt track at the bottom of the

dike. Charlie was better on flat ground, but not much. After fifty yards, he fell. The next time he fell, he threw up.

He only had two glass bottles with breath from Mrs. Wisdom's ironwood trees. Two. And it was already time for one of them.

Charlie staggered off the track and found himself face-down on soft earth. The dust seemed full of fiery sparks. Bad sign. He tried to blink them away.

Sugar dropped onto his knees beside him. "I'm carrying you, Charlie," he said, sliding his hands under Charlie's arms. "I'll get you to Mack."

"No. Bag," Charlie grunted. "Get it off."

As Sugar reached for the bag, stink swept over them, and they heard the sound of running feet.

Sugar dove onto his belly beside Charlie as a pack of six Gren flashed by. They wore animal skins and struggled as they ran, shoving and slashing like they hated each other. The cloud of reek trailed after them toward the stadium.

"No girls," Charlie muttered. He felt hot all over. "Why no girls?"

Sugar rose to his knees and slid Charlie's arms out of the bag's shoulder straps. Charlie was surprised at how heavy his arms were when they were limp and useless.

"They have a mother," Charlie added. His voice sounded funny inside his head. "So there could be girls."

"Maybe that's why," Sugar whispered, lifting the bag.

"Mrs. Wiz says these things are all envy, right? A selfish dude hates on his sons. Maybe the Mother doesn't want the competition."

Sugar opened the bag flap and reached inside. "What do you need in here? Knife? Bottles?"

Acid boiled up into Charlie's throat. A hammer jumped inside his head. "Panther," he said.

"You're scaring me, bro." Sugar pulled out one of the glass bottles. He held it up. "Medicine, right?" He shook it. "Lead heavy but there's nothing in it."

Charlie fought to raise his dead arm. He made one finger almost point. "Panther," he said again.

Across the track, the big cat was inching out of tall grass and stray cane, muscles taut beneath its fur, golden eyes wide.

Sugar turned and threw up his arms as the cat sprang across the track and slammed into him. They tumbled into the cane, and Charlie's eyes closed.

He heard the cat return. It gripped Charlie's shoulder at the base of his neck with its teeth and dragged him across the ground. His heels bounced, and his ankle hurt. Sugar was yelling again. The cat let go, and Charlie's head thumped against the ground.

Charlie found himself drifting toward something warmer and deeper than sleep. While his body's eyes were shut, some other eyes opened. He saw that he was lying on a vast bed of fiery sparks. The sparks tugged at him, stinging his ankle when they touched it. It would stop stinging soon. His sparks would join the others. He would be muck.

Smooth cold slid into his mouth. Like syrup without the sticky. If syrup could be as heavy as lead but made from air. If air could taste like silver and forests and stars and ice and years and years and years. If joy and lightning and glory and grief could be coiled up like a spring and dropped inside you.

Boom.

Charlie's nerves sharpened into crystals. His ankle screamed, but every other part of him was screaming, too. He was made of screaming. It was as if he were an arm or a leg that had grown numb, but now the blood was roaring back with an army of pricking needles. His eyes, his spine, his tongue, his throat—all of him tingled with the agony of returning life.

Sugar stood over him, holding an empty bottle. He was yelling, but his voice was nothing compared to the icebergs smashing inside Charlie's eardrums. Charlie slammed his arms against the ground and jumped to his feet. He shook. He rolled his shoulders and swung his arms and bounced. He twitched and shivered and kicked. The tingling was growing, and Charlie felt like he was going to explode. Like he was going to shriek off into the air like a firework and light fields on fire where he landed. He yelled and then yelled some more, and when he inhaled, it felt like his lungs were pressing against needles. Despite the pain, they wanted to keep filling, they wanted to expand until they splintered his ribs.

And then Charlie was still, his head was back, his face up. Hot tears slipped over his jaw and down his neck. The clouds had broken. He could see stars. He thought he knew what it must feel like to be one. He understood how a tree could spring up in a grave. If he died right here, with the breath of the ironwood in him, he knew another tree would come up for him.

"Charlie," Sugar said behind him. "Charlie, the panther . . ."

Charlie looked down. The panther stood directly in front of him. He realized he'd seen her eyes before, in a tree above him. He'd helped Cotton honor her fallen mate. She was Lio's.

The panther bit the hem of Charlie's shirt and tugged. Mrs. Wisdom had said that Lio's panther had been hunting the Mother with him. Lio's last panther.

"I have to go," Charlie said. He looked back at Sugar. His brother was wide-eyed and confused. Charlie's bag was on the ground between them. "Find Mack. Tell him everything—Mrs. Wisdom, Cotton, me, all those sick sleeping boys. And stay clear of the Stanks."

Charlie walked back to his bag, his legs shivering as he stepped, wanting to spring. He lifted the bag and slid it onto his shoulders.

"What's your real name?" Charlie asked his brother. "I should know."

Sugar bit his lip, almost objecting. Almost.

"Bobby," he said. "Bobby Reynolds Diaz. But don't you ever call me that."

Charlie nodded. "Thanks for finding me. And for . . . telling me." He was feeling a lot of things, impossible things, and most of them didn't have words. "I'm sorry that our dad . . . I'm sorry that he was like that. To you."

Sugar smiled, barely. "Wasn't roses on your end, either. I wouldn't trade."

"If I don't . . . if we don't . . ." Charlie stopped. The panther was nudging the back of his leg. "Tell my mom I love her. Tell Mack thanks for everything. And please be Molly's brother. She needs one. Everything I have is hers. Including you."

"Tell them yourself," Sugar said. "I'm coming with you."

But Charlie had already turned. He was running toward the stadium and Taper beyond it, matching strides with the panther loping beside him.

Sugar shouted and jumped forward. He dug in and lengthened his stride and chewed up the dirt track at his top speed, and still Charlie pulled away. Forty yards, and Sugar slowed, chest heaving.

Charlie was gone.

✳ ✳ ✳

Charlie was running at daydream speeds. Years before, when Mack would drive him to school, he'd press his head against the glass and imagine running alongside the car, leaping roads and mailboxes and pedestrians and cyclists as he kept pace. Daydream fast.

The panther turned into a field with waist-high cane. Charlie turned after him, ignoring the blades slashing his arms as his feet pummeled soft earth. They crossed a dirt road and the panther leapt a canal. Charlie planted and followed, arms swinging, floating too far, too high. The panther landed and turned. Charlie landed and tumbled into a wall of stalks.

The pain was like laughter. Like a joke between his already-throbbing ankle and the rest of his body. Charlie fought free and kept running.

A train mounded high with burned and diced sugar bones was rolling through the cane without lights, without bells or horns or warnings, clicking and sparking on tired rails. The panther turned and led Charlie alongside it, lengthening its stride. Charlie followed, the burning in his muscles ignored by something older and stronger and more stubborn. They were near the train engine, then they were pulling away, and the panther leapt the tracks.

Charlie was alive, and he was quick. Something inside him that had only ever whispered was roaring. Every spark in every cell of his body was firing. He was planting his left foot. He was turning in front of the train. He was jumping.

He was flying.

The engine slid behind him as he twisted in the air and landed. The panther was waiting. A gravel road ran between cane fields to a chain-link fence. Beyond the fence was the underbelly of shaking bleachers, beaten like drums by thousands of feet. Beyond that, white lights on green grass. Boys running in bright helmets.

Charlie could smell popcorn and hot dogs and pizza. He could smell fryers frying. But there was something else, too. Something much, much worse.

Charlie watched the panther accelerate, then rise up and over the fence. He watched her clear the line of cops on the other side, and saw them jolt in surprise and reach for their guns when she landed. And then Charlie was jumping. His hands grabbed the top bar and his legs swung to the side. He rotated and landed with hands up, facing the cops.

"Don't" was all he said. And he was running again.

Charlie followed the panther past an ambulance, past a marching band with dancers and cheerleaders and three drum majors with huge hats and massive scepter batons, all assembled and waiting for halftime.

Then he followed her out under the lights as she shot onto the field.

The crowd jumped to its feet, and Charlie saw the ball flying. He saw three players racing toward him with eyes up, tracking the ball. They didn't see him.

But the crowd did. There was a slow moment of pure silence. And then shrieks. Shock. Fear. Laughter.

The panther darted between the players, sending one of them tumbling. Charlie jumped the player as he rolled, spreading his legs above flailing cleats.

* * *

On the sideline, Sheriff Leroy Spitz tugged off his sun visor and leaned forward squinting. The ball was caught. The player scored. But no one cared. There was a boy chasing a panther—a *panther*—across the field. Spitz burst out laughing.

"Hell in a basket," Spitz said. "I told Mack that kid would show. I told him."

Hydrant pulled off his sunglasses. "He got some *speed*."

Spitz looked around. "Bobby should have been here for this. He shoulda seen his boy run, shoulda seen his boy *fly*."

Spitz laughed again as Charlie and the panther shot past the rest of the players, more than a few of them scrambling out of the way, and scattered the other school's band.

"I tell you what," Spitz said, settling his visor back onto his head. "Most boys chase rabbits."

Charlie followed the panther through a tunnel of shocked kids in baggy uniforms, holding horns and strapped to drums. He and the panther jumped another fence and the lights were behind them. Wisps of reek drifted around them and then were gone, clinging close to the stadium.

Away from people, the panther slowed to a trot, her head forward and low like she was hunting. Charlie didn't feel quite as springy as he had when they'd started. His lungs were heaving quickly, and pain was more noticeable underneath the cold, sharp burning life that had filled him.

They cut through Taper, jogging behind houses, hopping fences, disturbing dogs, avoiding nothing. Then Charlie could see the church.

The panther turned onto a road between a cane field and a canal that ran straight back toward the dark wall of the swamp. Charlie knew where they were going.

The panther quickened her pace, her tail stiff and her shoulders rocking but her head and neck always level with the ground. Charlie could feel her tension. Something was different in the fields. Something had changed, and not for the better.

The panther slipped off the road and padded through soft, thick muck cut bare between fields to control the burns. Road. Track. Ditch. Track. Canal bank. The panther was choosing her course carefully, sinking lower and lower to the ground as she went. Doubling back. Circling around.

Charlie didn't argue.

When they were right beside the swamp, dark trees jutting against the sky, she went into cane too dense for him to walk through.

As Charlie paused, a breeze rustled through the cane and the smell hit him like a fist. He dropped to his knees and stifled a gag. Now he knew why they'd been circling. They were downwind.

Holding his breath, he wormed into the cane, grateful that the wind would cover his rattling with its own.

The darkness under the leaves was total. His hands and knees sank inches into the cool, silty muck, too sheltered to have become mud in the rain. His hand found the panther's tail, and it twitched, thumping him in the face. Lowering himself onto his stomach, he slithered forward. Trying not to smell. Trying to ignore the resentments springing up in his mind:

Mack was Molly's real father. She had it so much better than Charlie ever would.

His mother would never stop being scared. He needed a mother who was brave.

Cotton was dying in some happy dream. Charlie was going to die in a nightmare.

Sugar was a football star.

As soon as he pushed one away, the next one would pop up. Anger. Hate. Self-pity. Anger. Just about every human on the planet was better off than Charlie at this moment. Every single one of them.

Charlie couldn't bite his brain, so he bit his lip. Not true, he thought. He adored Molly. He would die for Molly. He apologized to his mother in his head. He threw his arms around her and lifted her off the ground until she laughed. If she hadn't been brave, he wouldn't still be alive. Cotton had gotten hurt saving Charlie, and he wasn't going to die. Sugar should be a football star. He should be winning a game right now. But he'd given that up to look for a brother who'd known nothing about him.

Charlie saw light. Fire. He pulled his shirt up over his mouth and nose, then pressed his face between two cool stalks of cane. The panther was warm and solid against his shoulder. They had cut across the corner of the field and were looking at the trees. At the canal bank. At the mound that bridged it.

There were a dozen Gren at least. The muck on their skin was still wet. Every one of them was holding a torch. Every one of them held a weapon—clubs, hooks, claws, spikes, spears.

A tall, slender woman stood above them on the mound that dammed the canal, just beyond where the chalk death stone would be. She wore a fur hood and cloak that reached the ground, hiding all but her mouth in shadow. There was a man's body curled on the stone at her feet. Torchlight glistened on his dark skin. There was a broken sword beside his hand. A helmet lay on the ground beside his head.

Lio.

The woman spoke and it was like the voice came from behind her, like she was funneling wind and releasing it in the shape of vast but quiet words.

"The stone is broken. The lion soul has departed. I have killed the one you could not." The cane swayed. Charlie felt the panther whisper a growl beside him.

"My mounds will draw strength enough for you, my newborn sons, and many more to come." The wind grew and the voice with it. "Gather them for me." The torches flickered. The Gren stirred.

"Burn the church. Burn the fields. Make this your mother's holy place. Quiet every mouth but mine."

The wind swirled, and the cane with it.

"Your older brothers begin already. Go."

The Stanks opened their mouths in silent howls and then sprang away. Only one Gren remained, tall and broad and still. Shadow and darkness clung to him where the others had worn skins. Light avoided settling on his face. Charlie knew that he had seen that darkness before. He had smelled its stench. The Mother looked down at Lio. She pushed back her hood. Her hair was thick and straight and white, like ice spun into silk. Her face was pale underneath a spatter of freckles, like a thrown stain.

Charlie held his breath. He was looking at a version of Mrs. Wisdom, but taller, thinner, and without the softness or the goodness or the creases of age.

She nudged Lio with her toe.

"Bring him," she said. And as the shadowy Gren bent over Lio's body, she turned and disappeared into the swamp.

TWELVE

TRUCK

When Sugar came to a stop outside the stadium fence, the teams were already in the locker rooms for halftime and the first band was marching onto the field. Rows of girls in flowing gold pants led them, flags snapping and twirling in their hands.

The crowd was restless, angry, the mood wrong for halftime. Too few people laughing, too few heading for the concession stand. Sugar looked up at the scoreboard. The game was close. It didn't make sense.

The announcer's voice crackled through old speakers. "Behold! The ladies of elegance . . ."

Flags arced high and were caught again. Sugar scrambled up the fence and dropped inside. The whole place smelled like the bathrooms had overflowed, like Porta-Johns had been upended under the bleachers.

"Aren't they elegant?" the announcer asked as the crowd started raining insults down on the girls.

Sugar frowned and jogged toward the locker room. He needed to find a coach with a phone and Mack's number. On the opposite sideline, he saw two cheerleaders fighting. The others joined in. Then one of the flag girls turned and broke her flag across another girl's back. The music staggered and struggled. A trombone was kicking a saxophone. A bass drum knocked a smaller drum flat. In the bleachers, fights were breaking out. Someone was thrown over a rail.

All around, cops were springing into action, racing toward the brawlers. As they ran, Sugar saw a shorter fat cop pull his gun and shoot a faster lean cop in the leg. As the fat one passed the wounded man, he threw his hands in the air in triumph, like the winner of a race. He got a baton across the kneecaps for his trouble and tumbled to the turf.

At the far end of the field, beneath the scoreboard, Sugar saw Stanks pour over the fence and race across the grass toward the stands.

On the field, one little drummer was still drumming. Every other human in the stadium turned and tried to run.

Benches tumbled. Rails bent and broke.

Sugar sprinted for the locker rooms.

❋ ❋ ❋

Mack had turned off the road that ran through downtown Taper, and they were coming up on the stadium. The glow was just ahead. Soon, he would glimpse the scoreboard and the score of the first game that he should have been coaching. Soon, he would have to decide what to do next.

Natalie was now in the passenger seat beside him. Molly was awake in the back, writhing in her car seat, fighting straps and buckles.

Natalie began to sing quietly, and her voice made Mack ache. Molly calmed in the back. Her breathing grew slow and steady.

Mack's phone vibrated in his pocket. He dug it out and tossed it to Natalie. She looked at it and nodded, still humming. Mack pushed a button on the steering wheel and a voice barked through the car speakers.

"Mack?" It was the assistant coach.

"I'm here, Steve," Mack said. "You hear anything from Charlie?"

"Hear anything?" Steve said. "I *saw* him, and so did every other person in town. He chased a panther across the field just before halftime. A full-grown panther, Mack. Sugar turned up, too, and he's trying to tell me some crazy story about monsters and dead people and all sorts of stuff I don't have time to hear."

Natalie grabbed Mack's hand. "He's all right? Charlie's all right?"

"Don't know about that," Steve said. "Depends on

whether he caught that panther. Pray he didn't, I guess. He's gone now."

"We're outside the stadium," Mack said. They were approaching the parking lot, and passed a checkpoint and four cop cars with their lights spinning. But no cops in sight. "Get back to the guys. I'll be there in two ticks."

"No!" Steve said. "Stay in your car. Steer clear. That's why I was calling. There's a riot going in the stadium, man. Chaos. We're locked inside the locker room. Big Surge is holding the door. I . . . ev—" Steve's voice was swallowed up by shouting.

Mack turned into the parking lot and stopped. People were flooding over destroyed turnstiles, fighting on the roof of the concession stand. Boys were standing on cars, stomping in windshields. A few of them looked up at Mack's headlights. They jumped off and started toward them.

Mack threw the car in reverse and backed into the road. He spun the car around, shifted, and punched the gas.

Molly began to cry.

"Steve!" Mack yelled.

"Getting rough in here," Steve crackled. "Couple hurt. Idiot kids."

"Did Sugar say where Charlie was going? Did he have any idea?"

"To kill some mother," Steve said. "But mostly he's jabbering about Stanks or Grens or something and how they're making everyone crazy. Hey, hey, hey! No! You two shut your mouths—"

The line went dead.

Mack stepped on the brakes. *Gren* . . . He'd heard that word. Like everyone who'd been a kid in the muck, he'd heard some crazy stories. And he'd had dreams that Mrs. Wisdom had blamed on the moon. On the wind. Or some smell.

There was a memory in his mind somewhere, blurry and distant. A bad memory.

A panther. He knew who had panthers. That much was encouraging.

"Mack?" Natalie's face was stone. Mack called it her game face.

"You have your phone?" Mack asked. His wife nodded as she handed his back. Mack kissed her. He kissed his fingers and twisted around to rub them on Molly's cheek in the backseat. "Lock the doors and keep moving. Stay on the edge of town, but in the light. I might need a ride in a hurry. Don't let anyone near the car. Not even cops. No one."

"What are you going to do?"

Mack opened his door and stepped into the road. "Charlie was just here. Wait for my call."

Natalie slid over the console between the seats and dropped in behind the steering wheel. Her eyes were wide, but her jaw was set. She nodded. Mack kissed her again and shut the door. Molly watched him as the Rover rolled away.

Two hundred yards behind him, cop cars were being smashed. He could hear the helicopter returning.

Mack left the road, hopped a ditch, and cut through the tall grass, jogging toward the stadium.

※ ※ ※

Charlie had watched the Mother disappear. He had watched the one remaining Gren grab Lio's body by the ankle and drag it through the brush after her.

The stink had lessened, but it wasn't gone. And so he had held still, the panther beside him. But he wasn't here to hide. He was here to find. To hunt.

And then he heard it—cane crackling behind him. He looked over his shoulder and saw stripes of red fire between the stalks. The stink suddenly grew and quick, muddy feet with jagged toes slid around the corner of the field. A rough hand was plunging a torch into the low cane leaves as the feet ran.

The panther slipped quickly forward and out of the field. Charlie flinched back, deeper into the cane.

The torch dove in beneath his face and then was gone. Dry leaves sprang into fiery life and quickly formed a wall. Heat billowed around Charlie as the cane popped and the wet leaves above him hissed and steamed.

Charlie wasn't a rabbit, he couldn't run from this. He

threw his arms over his face and plunged through the fire, tumbling onto the road beside the canal.

Farther down the road, the Stank with the torch had stopped and was watching him. He was wearing a hood of skunks and rats and snakes over baggy mud-caked jeans. He was skinny. Young. In one hand he held the torch, and in the other a long wooden spike.

With a start, Charlie realized his shorts were on fire. He jumped to his feet and slapped them out.

Across the fields, over by the church, he heard shouts and then a gun fired twice. A third time. Charlie looked around and saw that this was not the only field burning. Everywhere, smoke and steam were rising. The tallest flames of all were licking the church.

The young Stank bent his knees and crept slowly forward, as if Charlie couldn't see him.

Charlie backed away, unslinging his bag. "I can see you. I can. You're not sneaking up on me." He pulled the long bone knife out of the cloth and out of his bag. It was hot against his skin.

Charlie dropped the bag and slid a little closer to the canal. "Come on!" he shouted. "Do I need a red cloth or something? Let's go!"

Between two heartbeats, the young Stank charged.

Charlie had a simple plan. Drop to the ground. Kick the Gren with both feet. Flip him into the canal. He managed to drop onto his back. The Gren raked the torch across his bare shins and stepped around Charlie's kick. He plunged the thick spike down at Charlie's chest. Charlie twisted clear of the blow, shoving the bone knife up at the Stank's mud-covered stomach.

An engine roared and lights flashed. The Stank turned as a red truck with lights lining its roll bar bounced out from between two fields and slid almost to the canal. The driver jumped out and climbed onto the roof of the cab. He was wearing a denim jacket and a trucker's cap. A shotgun was strapped to his shoulder, and he carried a hunting rifle with a scope. Long, stringy hair hung out of the back of his hat.

He aimed and fired back into the fields at something Charlie couldn't see. Aimed and fired. Aimed and fired. The Gren above Charlie snarled and ran at the lights and the noise.

"Look out!" Charlie shouted as the Gren leapt onto the hood. The man spun and his rifle cracked. The Gren tumbled to the ground, his fur hood snagging on the truck's fender. The man turned and fired again, back into the field.

Charlie ran forward. He grabbed the still-moving Stank by the ankles and dragged him out of his hood, toward the canal. Without the rotting animal skins, the Stank was suddenly very human—a filthy, skinny teenage boy, furious and confused.

"I'm sorry this happened to you," Charlie said. "You didn't want it, and if you did, you shouldn't've."

The Stank saw the water and his confusion disappeared. He jerked a foot free and kicked Charlie in the jaw. He twisted onto his hands and knees and tried to run, but Charlie landed on his back. He hugged the young Gren's arms tight to his sides and drove his face into the ground.

"I saw her," Charlie said. "She's not your mother."

The boy twisted and kicked but Charlie held on.

"The water will take it away. It will all stop. You won't belong to her."

The man on the truck was shouting and his gun was firing and fields were burning, but all Charlie cared about was one boy who didn't have to be a monster.

The Gren stopped fighting, his body seeming to shake with the effort. Then, as quiet as a ghost, he gasped one word into the earth.

"Please."

Charlie rolled with him over the bank and into the canal.

In the cool water, Charlie let go. His feet found the bottom and he kicked up to the surface. The boy surfaced beside him. He didn't speak. He didn't claw for the bank like the old man had. He looked at Charlie. His eyes were at peace. And then they closed.

Metal crunched and screamed. The red truck slid sideways toward the canal—the Gren were flipping it. The man on the roof jumped for the water as the truck rolled up and over.

Charlie grabbed a breath and dove. Bright lights on a roll bar exploded past his face. The cab roof slammed him down, pinned his legs to a log, and pinned the log to the bottom.

A gator wriggled out from underneath the log, jerking and thrashing to get its tail free. Charlie felt its back against his own, its claws against his arm, and then it was gone. But he wasn't.

I'd rather die than not try.

Charlie bubbled his lungs empty. He fought, but fighting was pointless. It was a truck. He stared past his legs at the lights, wondering how long they would keep shining. He already wanted them off. So he shut his eyes.

✳ ✳ ✳

Mack crouched in the shadows next to the bleachers. Most of the fans were gone, and those who weren't were tangled in the bleachers or sprawled on the ground.

An awful reek floated across the turf like cold air. When it reached him, Mack's skin tightened and disgust washed through him. This stupid town and all its petty people deserved everything they were getting. Disgust boiled toward anger, but Mack was already closing iron fists of self-control around the first surprise attack of feeling.

He'd had a lot of practice. This was game time, and he never played angry. When other men cracked, he was a rock. When opponents burned with fiery rage, Mack was searing cold. He could find clarity and yawn calm even when a hundred thousand people were screaming at him and cameras were in his face, spying for tens of millions more.

Mack stayed focused.

The helicopter was hovering over the field, scanning it with its spotlight, which was pointless with the stadium lights on. A group of cops—traffic, state troopers, gang-unit guys in fatigues and flak jackets, maybe fifteen in all—had circled up with backs together on the far sideline. They were terrified and arguing, but one man in fatigues seemed to be in some sort of control, his dark shaved head glistening and his booming orders drowning out complaints and arguments.

Fast dark shapes with bare feet and fur hoods moved fluidly through the bleachers above the cops. More danced past them in the grass, reversing direction just before a gun fired, darting in and slashing at legs and tumbling away again.

Mack turned and looked toward the locker room. He hoped Steve still had the boys inside, and that they were all still sane.

A cold gun barrel tapped him on the back of the neck.

"Winner, winner, chicken dinner," Spitz said behind him. "My night might look up after all."

Mack rose slowly, hands up, and turned. Spitz looked

bad. His visor was gone and he had a lump on his forehead ready to hatch into something the size of a turkey. His nose was broken, and while the bleeding had stopped, it had already turned his mustache into a fat, hairy scab. His pants were torn and sagging.

"Leroy, what are you doing?" Mack said. He gestured at the group of cops near the bleachers. "Why aren't you with them?"

"Them," Spitz said. "Those fools. Hydrant is with them. *Them* is where every mindless numbskull like you should be. I'm with *me*."

"Hiding under the bleachers?" Mack asked. "People need your help, Spitz."

Spitz waggled his gun. "Oh, shut up. How many millions of dollars did you get to play football? How many parties and cars and houses?"

Mack didn't answer.

"Know how many I got?" Spitz asked. "Zero. Zeeeer to the O. Want to explain to me how that's fair?" He leaned forward, pressing the gun against Mack's forehead. "You can't, because it ain't."

Mack snatched the barrel, twisted the gun out of Spitz's hand, and punched him in the stomach. The sheriff doubled over, gasping.

"You're under . . . arrest."

"Maybe later," Mack said. He checked the revolver's

171

chambers. Fully loaded. Mack gritted his teeth. Charlie had been here, and Mack wasn't leaving until he was sure that Charlie wasn't hunkered down hurt and hiding, or worse.

Mack crossed the sideline and angled toward the locker rooms behind the goalpost.

"Hey!" Spitz shrieked behind him. "Monsters! Here's one! Get him!"

※　※　※

Charlie opened his eyes. Above him were the branches of scruffy trees. Fire glowed nearby. Mountains of smoke were crawling into the night sky, but the wind was bending it away, carrying it toward the sea. Charlie could see the moon. And stars.

He sat up slowly. He was very wet, and his head hurt. His leg was heavy and throbbing, especially his ankle. He was lying on the mound that bridged the canal and ran into the swamp. The red truck was upside down in the canal in front of him. Across the smoldering fields, he could see the church burning.

Charlie glanced down. He was sitting on the chalk stone.

He jerked away, scrambling off it like a crab. The stone had changed. It was all splinters. They were soft, breaking down to powder between his fingertips.

Under the trees, a small flame flicked to life. The man

172

from the truck was trying to light a cigarette. His face was wet. Long hair clung to his cheeks. The trucker cap was missing.

"Nice trick with the water." He exhaled. "Enough bullets stop 'em, too. For a while." He held up the lighter. "Hope you don't mind. It was in your bag. You shouldn't be smoking anyway."

"It wasn't for smoking," Charlie said. "Who are you and what do you want?"

The man laughed. "Right to the point, even when the world's trying to end. I like that." He held up Charlie's bag and dropped the lighter inside, then tossed it to him. Charlie caught it in his lap.

"I'm the man who just saved your life, Charlie." He gave up on his cigarette and flicked it away. He smiled. "I'm your father, and don't you forget it."

THIRTEEN
WOMB

Charlie stood with his back to a tree and his pack hanging in front of his chest. His eyes were sweeping the shadows under the trees for any sign of the panther. She kept disappearing and then reappearing to tug on Charlie's shirt once she was certain of the trail. But this last time, she hadn't returned.

There had been no sign or smell of any Gren.

Charlie's mind was more crowded than it had ever been, more overloaded with worries and wonders and confusions than he had energy to think about. Cotton was dying. He had just met his father for the first time since his father had earned a trip to prison. But more importantly, Charlie wasn't feeling well at all. His leg was throbbing up to the knee. He'd dry-heaved into the bushes. His eyes weren't focusing.

Charlie didn't have much time, and he knew it.

Bobby Reynolds, an older, thicker, lumpier-faced version of the man Charlie had once loved and feared, crashed through the brush, up to his knees in watery mud.

Animals were shrieking at Charlie from the leafy darkness above. Whatever they were, Charlie didn't like them.

"Mound curls north," Bobby said. "Joins one that shoots southwest. Hand me that map."

Charlie passed over Cotton's paper. Bobby used the lighter to look at it.

His father had only been interested in two things. First, helping his son and keeping him safe—especially if that meant putting down swamp monsters. And second, completely ignoring the past and acting like nothing had happened that he might need to address.

Charlie was glad. The last thing he wanted was a talk. A talk would tear things loose inside him he couldn't deal with right now. On any other night, the idea of being alone with his father would have terrified him. Not tonight. Tonight, Bobby Reynolds was way down the list of scary things. For that, Charlie was grateful.

Charlie leaned his head against a tree trunk. He was feeling ill again.

"North," his father grunted. He tucked the map into the pocket of his denim jacket. "At least if you want to follow these mounds to the middle."

Charlie didn't leave the support of his tree. He just held out his hand for the map.

"You don't trust me," his father said.

Charlie didn't answer. He didn't lower his hand.

"Right," said Bobby Reynolds. "Old memories of good old dad, huh? Well, I spent the last couple days looking for you. I just killed—or rekilled—four of those things, and then I pulled you out from under my truck and saved your pasty hide. Now I'm taking you on your crazy swamp quest, and the last time I checked, Prester Mack isn't here. So start trusting."

He slapped the map into Charlie's hand. Charlie followed him through the swamp slop, pushed through brush, and then once again found solid mound ground beneath his feet.

Something moved in the darkness ahead. Charlie's father clamped his big hand on Charlie's shoulder.

"Panther," Bobby whispered. He raised his rifle.

"Really?" Charlie shrugged out of his father's grip and staggered forward. The panther was pacing—climbing a fallen tree, descending, dropping onto the narrow mound and sliding through brush, circling a small pool of black mud, hopping back onto the mound, climbing the tree, and back down again.

Moonlight trickled through the trees, but there was no way to recognize the panther for sure. Except that it hadn't attacked them.

"She's mine," Charlie said, and as he moved forward, he understood her frustration. The mound was blocked with a tangle of branches and trunks so tight that she couldn't get through—so tight that it couldn't be natural. It was like the wall of a stockade, but jumbled and jagged and leaning out over you when you got close to it.

Charlie held out his hand and let his fingers drag down the panther's body as she passed. He shut his eyes and tried not to feel dizzy.

"We're here," he said. "But how do we get in?"

Charlie's father stood beside him. "There's a way. Over or under or through, they get in somehow."

"No way they climb better than a panther," Charlie said. "And she's confused." He thought about that Gren dragging Lio by the ankle, about that woman. They weren't scrambling over walls like monkeys.

The Gren were connected to the muck. They were caked with it. Later on, if the Mother had her way, they would be dragging dozens of bodies back into this swamp. She would be birthing more sons. She had a front door somewhere. Charlie just needed to see one of the Gren use it. Then he would go in and pull his bone knife and . . . well, he didn't want to think about that part.

Charlie dug into his bag and pulled out his air horn.

"Knock, knock," he said. And he squeezed the trigger.

His father grabbed him from behind and tore the horn out of his hand. The enormous blast of sound died just as suddenly as it had begun. The panther was staring at him.

"Are you crazy?" his father hissed.

"Hopefully, a Stank will come from inside, not from behind us." He pointed at the pool of mud. "I'm guessing right there. It looks just like they smell."

His father handed back the air horn and raised his rifle. While they watched, it stirred.

Two huge hands reached up out of the goop and grabbed a log. Shadow raced toward them, clinging to the dripping arms. Head and shoulders followed, slick with muck, and blanketed with thickening darkness.

Charlie's father fired, and the snarling panther leapt onto the Gren's back before its ribs cleared the slop. Charlie sat down and closed his eyes. He didn't want to watch, and he didn't want to think about what came next. He was all the way up the high dive now, and there was no turning back.

"Charlie?" his father asked.

Charlie groaned, opened his eyes, and stood up.

"You don't have to do this," his father said. "I'll take you back to your mother. Or you could just climb a tree with your panther and sleep."

Charlie shook his head. "I do have to do this. If I don't . . ."

"I have a gun. I'll do it."

Charlie limped over to the edge of the muck. The panther had dragged the Gren's body to the other side of the mound and left it in a swamp puddle. It was only a few inches deep. Not enough to keep him dead, but it was better than nothing.

"Charlie?"

Charlie looked at his father. Really looked. This was it. This could be his last chance to say what needed saying. His memories were roaring and tumbling and confused. The man was like an illustration from painful stories in his mind. It was strange that he was real. That he still existed after that final awful night.

Charlie blinked slowly. Bobby Reynolds. His dad. Standing in the moonlight next to him, pretending like they were friends, like they had always been on the same team.

"You were the monster," Charlie said. "You hurt Mom. You hurt me. You hurt Sugar. You hurt Sugar's mom."

His father frowned. "I did my time," he said. "I paid."

"No, Dad." Charlie shook his head. His body felt fuzzy, but his mind was hot and clear. "You didn't. You owed us *you*. All of you. And you owed Sugar and Sugar's mom. You belonged to us, but all you did was hate us for it."

Charlie could see his father's cheeks twitch. He had forgotten that they did that. He mostly remembered the eyes and the hands.

He could see the anger coming.

"You think you understand?" his father asked.

"Stop it," Charlie said. "It won't help. I don't hate you,

okay? I used to. And I'm sorry about that. It made everything worse."

Charlie looked down at the muck pool beside the low mound. "Think there are more in there? Should I blow my horn again?"

His father didn't answer. Instead, he took one step toward the pool, hugged his rifle to his chest, and jumped in.

The splash sounded more like a slap. He was gone. The panther jumped forward and then back again. She danced around the pool.

"I like you, lady cat." Charlie rubbed her head and scratched behind her ears. "Don't let me come back out if I'm wearing rotten skin."

Charlie took a deep breath, and then chickened out. He tried another, added a step, and then hopped away sideways instead of into the muck pool. The third time, he said his goodbyes to the world and jumped as high as he could over the slop. He squeezed his bag tight and kept his legs straight and together.

The muck swallowed him.

Charlie tried to kick. He tried to swim. It was like trying to swim through sand—too thick for his limbs to move easily, too thin for his hands to grab and pull. But he was moving, barely. Then his fingers found a root. He grabbed it and pulled himself forward and groped for another, then another. His chest wanted to collapse. He tried to exhale, but the muck wouldn't let him.

He knew he was out when he could spit. He clawed mud off his eyes and blew it out his nose. His hands found a solid bank and he wriggled onto it. It was sharp everywhere, and when he'd blinked enough, he could see why. It was made entirely of crushed shells.

A hand grabbed him between the shoulder blades and pulled him to his feet. It was his father, looking chocolate-dipped.

Charlie looked around. The place was like an enormous cave, fifty yards long or even longer, but the walls and ceiling were wood—branches and trunks woven tight. Torches lined the walls, and there were no openings anywhere. The floor was shattered shells mounded into paths that wound between and around dozens of pools of muck like the one they had just climbed through.

Charlie limped forward. In the center of the room, there was a fountain. Like the floor, the fountain rim was made of shattered shells, but these shells were swirling slowly with the water they held, clicking and rasping against each other as they did. In the center, shell shards formed the shape of a tall woman. While Charlie watched, the shape clattered into a serpent, a dragon, a man, a dog. Swamp water burbled out of the constantly changing shard statue, and streamed down its sides into the pool below.

"Do not touch it." The voice was wind, and the torches flickered with each word.

At the far end of the hall, thick shadow suddenly lifted, and Charlie was looking at the Mother seated on a shell throne, inside another fountain pool. She was clothed in white feathers and black furs, and water flowed around her. Lio's body floated and drifted at her feet.

Weapons hung on the wooden walls that curved around the fountain throne. Ancient swords encrusted with jewels and rust, bows, muskets, spears, sabers, cutlasses, rifles. There were too many to count, all displayed on the walls like trophies.

Charlie started toward her, as stable as he could manage. His father followed.

"Life flows in," the Mother said, and she pushed back her dark fur hood. Firelight seemed to drip from her silver hair. "Welcome. The fountain must feed. The more she feeds, the more she gives."

Charlie wound his way between pools of muck and stopped twenty feet from her throne. Behind him, Bobby Reynolds cleared his throat.

"What does the fountain do?"

The Mother smiled, creasing the stain of freckles on her cheeks. "For you? It would give you strength and speed and hunger. It would make you run as you have never run. It would make you young enough to play your game again."

Charlie shot a look at his father, then turned back to the Mother.

"My cousin is dying because of your mounds and Stanks and probably your fountain, too."

"As are you," the Mother said.

"Yeah, well." Charlie shrugged. "Not if I kill you first."

The Mother laughed. "You would kill an old woman while her sons are away?"

Charlie nodded. "Seems like the best time."

"Have you brought a weapon for my collection?" the Mother asked. "I am afraid I only hang the arms of heroes. Who told you to try this foolish thing?"

"Nobody. But Mrs. Wisdom didn't think it was an awful idea."

"Mrs. Wisdom." The Mother sneered when she said it. "She was my granddaughter once, but she has always been a fool. Never more so than when she chose that man for herself. She took after her father's line."

Charlie's father checked his muck-slathered rifle. Then he fished a bullet out of his jeans and slid it in.

"You think lifeless lead will reach me?" the Mother asked. "Do you think any metal could? Any soulless stone? Any curse? Fire if you like. Take up a weapon from the wall. Try to strike me down. If you are strong, I will make you one of my sons. If you are weak, I will feed you to them."

Charlie pulled the bone knife out of his muddy bag. His father raised his rifle.

The Mother held up her wet hand, and her fingers were taloned like a vulture's. The bone knife suddenly jumped toward her, dragging Charlie behind it. His father fired and the gun exploded in his hands, knocking him backward.

Charlie let go of the knife and fell on his face, clipping his chin on the shell floor.

The Mother laughed and the fountain behind Charlie geysered water almost to the ceiling; the swirling and rattling shells grew into a giant.

"This is my home!" she roared. "My womb, where I have birthed men mightier than Nimrod and Shamgar and Ishmael, where the earth feeds me the sparks of thousands and my fountain overflows with life."

Charlie scrambled toward the wall of weapons. His father got there first, pulled down an ax and a sword, and then ran straight at the Mother, snarling through gritted teeth.

Charlie saw the Mother rise from her seat and catch the sword in her bare hand. The steel shattered. Her other hand closed around the ax blade, talons punching through thick metal and scattering the shards like pottery.

Bobby Reynolds tried to use his fists.

The Mother toyed with him, carving him with one talon at a time, inflicting pain like a malicious cat that leaves its prey alive.

Charlie stared at the wall of weapons while his father screamed behind him. *No lifeless metal, no soulless stone. It* meant something. Something he should already know. Something he already felt inside him.

And then he saw it—between a scimitar and a spear with a blade like a scythe. It was a sword almost as tall as he was, and it had been carved from a single piece of wood. Grain swirled on the wide blade. The hilt was thick and long enough for three hands. Charlie tugged it down and nearly dropped it, surprised by the weight. It wasn't just wood. It was ironwood.

He turned as the Mother closed her taloned fist on his father's chest. With one hand, she picked him up and threw him against the wall. Weapons rained down around him. Charlie ran at her back. He raised the sword to his shoulder. He swung. She turned, smiling, and reached for his arcing blade.

Her talons shattered when she caught it. Her arm broke. She tumbled backward. Charlie didn't stop swinging. Not when she put the bone knife into his thigh. Not when needle talons gripped his calf. Not when his vision blurred and the world became sparks. He was swinging at white-hot flame, sparks stolen and hoarded like gold, and as he swung, they scattered.

Panting, Charlie felt his vision clear. He was facedown on wet shells. His limbs were lead. Every part of him was screaming in pain.

Not far from him, a battered pile of white feathers and fur was crawling toward the central fountain, now burbling quietly. Underneath the feathers, Charlie could see only vapor, a woman made of steam.

What had Mrs. Wisdom said? *Burning is the only way for her. She's died a dozen times and it never stuck. If you get her down, light her up like cane.*

Charlie's bag was under his body. He couldn't let her get to the fountain. He bullied himself up onto his shoulder and groped inside his bag. He found the lighter. For what felt like years, he tried to get his thumb to flick it. Finally, the flame came to life. He tried to calm his pounding heart. He ignored his throbbing head. If he missed, if the Mother made it into the fountain that the mounds fed with muck life . . .

Charlie pulled in a long breath and held it. Leaning on one elbow, he lobbed the flaming lighter at the crawling pile of feathers. End over end the little fire spun.

And then it landed. Like a pink flare in a cane field.

Nothing. And then smoke. Stink. Crackle. A scream made of hissing wind. Blaze. Heat found Charlie's face and he knew there was something else he was supposed to do. He pulled a bone knife out of his thigh and threw it on the fire. He couldn't watch. His arm couldn't hold him up. He fell onto his back, and as steam and smoke swirled above him, he shut his eyes and prayed that Cotton could still wake up. That the Gren would sleep in death without their Mother to feed them.

Charlie's eyes almost didn't open again. His world

ended. His mind saw nothing and knew nothing. Not darkness. Not lightness. Nothing.

The shell fountain and the shell throne collapsed, splashing and clattering like sea glass. Cool water washed across the floor, swallowing Charlie and spinning him around like driftwood. His world returned, his mind woke, and when he opened his eyes, he found himself staring at his father.

Bobby Reynolds was slumped against the wall. He looked like he was sleeping but his skin was far more pale. He had never looked angry when he slept and he didn't look angry now.

Charlie wormed his way to his father's side and pulled a small glass bottle from his bag. It looked empty, but it was heavy. Charlie tugged the cork free and shoved the bottle between his father's lips.

After a moment, Charlie's eyes shut and his arm fell. He didn't hear the glass bottle break.

Bobby Reynolds did.

＊ ＊ ＊

It was Sugar who found them between two smoldering fields. Before he'd died, Bobby had carried his son all the way from the swamp to just past the burned-out church. The doctor who performed Bobby's autopsy knew that wasn't possible, not with a collapsed lung and a ruptured aorta—and that was just to start. But nobody cared what the doctor said. Everyone knew that none of the week's events had been possible. Apparently, no one had informed the world. . . .

Bobby and Charlie had both reeked, and they had both been caked with dried swamp muck—all but Charlie's face, where it had been licked clean by a panther.

Mrs. Wisdom had asked Mack and Natalie if she could spend some time alone with Charlie in the hospital, and they had both agreed. Things looked better and better after her visit until the doctor finally said Charlie could keep recovering at home. And that was when the Macks noticed that they didn't really have a home, but the beach was close enough for now.

More than a dozen lost boys found their way back to Taper over the next couple days. They all told strange, confusing stories about tree forts and dreams, but the strangest belonged to Cotton Mack. People actually believed him.

Most people in Taper had trouble remembering the football riot accurately, although almost everyone said that they'd been there, and when they looked at the damage to the stadium, everyone agreed that more people should have been hurt than actually were.

Flags flew at half-mast for a week in honor of Sheriff Leroy Spitz, who died of a heart attack after trying to climb a fence out of the stadium during the riot.

Since the church had burned and needed rebuilding,

folks who remembered things remembered the bell that had fallen down through the floor and into the muck. And the people with memories told people with shovels, and they dug that bell up. And when the mound got itself a new white church to sit up on top, it came with a brand-new steeple. But the bell that rang inside it was older than Taper itself.

FOURTEEN

BEACH

Charlie and Cotton and Sugar sat in white chairs by a pool, watching palm trees bend beside the sea. They were still wearing ties from a funeral, and bandages from before that.

Mack was at a barbecue, slicking sauce on chicken with a paintbrush. Sugar's stepdad stood beside him—shorter and thicker and slower and balder and more mustached than Mack, but full of smiles and laughs that came out like gifts that he would never need back because he always had more.

He'd made the sauce.

"Wait till you taste it," Sugar said. "Seriously. There's nothing like it."

Charlie's mom and Sugar's mom and Cotton's mom were listening to Mrs. Wisdom and laughing just inside the glass doors of the beach house, and the boys all suspected that they were talking about them. But nobody said anything.

Cotton nodded at a stack of books that his mother had brought for Charlie's recovery.

"Don't worry, coz. I slipped a couple good ones in there. Don't go near that book by Dickens. He has better. But you have to read that edition of *Beowulf.*"

"Why?" Sugar asked.

"Because I've read three and it's the truest to the original Anglo-Saxon," Cotton said. "Serious awesome sauce."

Charlie smiled.

"No, I meant why read it at all?" Sugar asked. "It's poetry, right?"

Cotton sat up straight. His eyebrows went up. "You kidding me, coz?"

"I'm not your coz."

"You're my cousin's bro," Cotton said. "And any bro to my coz is a coz of mine. It's like relational math, *coz.* Simple."

Charlie burst out laughing. Sugar smiled. Cotton rolled on.

"And yeah, *Beowulf* is poetry, but it's poetry that's all blood and dragons and monsters. Think Vikings, but tougher." Cotton shook his head. "History of the world, *coz,* warriors and kings and conquerors, man, they ate poems up. I mean, ninjas even had haiku. You more manly than ninjas, Sugar Diaz?"

Sugar glanced at Charlie and then smirked at Cotton. "That all something your mom told you?"

Cotton groaned. "Always with the mom. And no, it's something anyone who knows the history of the world could tell you."

"Okay," Charlie said. He held up his hands. "I'm sold. Sugar, I'll let you know how it is."

Molly raced out of the house wearing inflated water wings so big her arms stuck almost straight out from her sides. She climbed onto the arm of Charlie's chair and dropped knees first at his stomach. He caught her before impact.

She raised both hands and widened her eyes.

"Monsters," she whispered.

"Nah," Cotton said. "Charlie killed those."

"Get in the water," Charlie said. "They don't like water."

So Molly did.

As the sun set over the Gulf of Mexico, two half brothers, one half sister, one step–second cousin, three moms, one former foster mother, and two stepdads raised glasses of wine and water and milk and cran-apple juice and root beer to the memory of a man who had hurt most of them.

But even out of him, good had come.

And when the sun did set and the moon rose, and the guests left that big white beach house and her husband was reading a book to her daughter, Natalie Mack wrapped herself in a sweater and walked out on the beach.

Her son limped after her. He put his arms around her while the wind pulled at the blond hair piled on her head, and he saw that her freckles were wet.

"Mom," Charlie said, "I don't know that I've ever thanked you."

She looked at him. "For what?"

"For keeping me safe when it was bad. For Mack. For Molly."

She leaned against him.

"For everything," he said.

And like a younger Mrs. Wisdom, she kissed him on the head.

EPILOGUE

Charlie Reynolds sprinted onto the field and didn't slow down until he reached the huddle. He heard his mom's sharp whistle. He heard Molly call his name. And then the huddle broke and he ran to his position split out wide by the sideline.

Sugar stood not ten yards from him, wearing his college hoodie.

"Speed, bro," Sugar said. "You got it."

Cotton was assessing the defense before bending down behind the center. He was cupping his hands and shouting down the line, pretending to call an audible. He loved doing that, but right now Mack only allowed him one audible per quarter.

"Twain! Twain!" Cotton shouted. "451 Bradbury!"

The other school's fans had started their slow chant back up.

"Homeschool . . . Homeschool . . . Homeschool . . ."

Cotton loved that, too. He was done with his act. He slid under the center. Charlie's eyes were on the ball. It snapped back into Cotton's hands, and Charlie exploded off the line. He jab-stepped in, slapped his defender's arms away, and then looped outside and accelerated. Another defender was racing over to help. Charlie heard the crowd inhale. He looked up and saw the ball high in the lights. It was soaring. Too deep.

Inside, Charlie scrambled for another gear, a gear his body knew was possible, an echo of the speed he had once felt when he was younger and the muck was new beneath his feet.

He found it. His legs churned. The teeth on the bottoms of his shoes barely touched down, but they tore the earth. He was flying now, pulling away from boys who wore a different color.

The crowd was on its feet, but Charlie only saw the ball. Thousands of voices unified in one growing swell of expectation, but Charlie only heard his own breathing.

He dove, and floated through the air like he was made of sparks.

Because he was.

GRATITUDE

Thanks to my lovely Heather Linn, who kept the spark of this story alive for too many years, and to Rory D, who devoured the first manuscript.

Thanks also to Liza McFadden, the Barbara Bush Foundation, and Celebration of Reading for all they have done for literacy, and for getting my feet planted in Florida for the first time.

Thanks to Judy Sanchez and U.S. Sugar for toting me out into the cane harvest and letting me play with fire while getting in the way of their amazing operation.

Thanks to Mary Ford for getting me onto the Pahokee sideline for the Muck Bowl.

Thanks to Captain Dan for the Swamp Boatery, and to Dane for falling in amongst the baby gators.

Thanks to my pops for first introducing me to *Beowulf* and the growling rhythms of Anglo-Saxon, and for his own brilliant verse-rendering.

Thanks to the rabbits.

Thanks to the runners.

Thanks to the One who invented quick and fire and heat, who beats the hearts and sends the breeze.

(Oh, and to Jim Thomas, because something tells me we have not yet begun to fight. . . .)

N. D. WILSON is the bestselling author of the Books of the 100 Cupboards, the Ashtown Burials series, and *Leepike Ridge*. Once, in the fourth grade, he split his buddy's arrow while shooting at a mattress from twenty yards. Now he writes at the top of a tall, skinny house, where he lives with a blue-eyed girl he stole from the ocean, their five young explorers, two tortoises, and one snake. For more information, please visit ndwilson.com.

DATE DUE

PRINTED IN U.S.A.